"Howdy, m... something...

Johnny tipp... his eyes. The... was an ardent fan.

"We're lost, and it's my sister's fault. I'm Marci Hamilton and that's my sister, Sissy." She pointed at the redhead.

"I'm..." At the last minute he decided to go with his middle name. "Johnny Walker."

"Johnny Walker?"

"My daddy had a good sense of humor," he said.

"Well, Johnny Walker, could you tell us how to get back to town? Any town will do, although one with a Dairy Queen would be nice."

"Yes, ma'am. In fact, I can do you one better. If you ladies will stay here, I'll ride back and get my pickup. Then you can follow me."

Johnny refused to acknowledge his racing pulse and clammy hands. Was he having a heart attack or had he fallen for a total stranger? It had been so many years since he'd felt anything even vaguely similar, he wasn't sure *what* was going on.

Whatever it was, this woman was enticing and he hadn't been tempted in a very long time. And best of all, she didn't recognize him.

Hot damn! Maybe it was his lucky day.

Dear Reader,

You are cordially invited to join Marci (MeeMaw) Hamilton and Sissy (Aunt Sissy) Aguirre on the road trip of a lifetime. Armed with a cherry-red T-Bird convertible, fancy cowboy boots and an award-winning barbecue sauce recipe, the sisters are off to win a series of cook-offs sponsored by country-and-western music icon J. W. (Johnny Walker) Watson. One look at the blonde in the convertible (Marci) and Johnny is smitten.

The sisters' adventures take them to the heart of the Texas country music scene, and Marci is having a ball enjoying the company of the sexiest, funniest, most appealing man she's ever met. She's head over heels in love, and that's a miracle considering her last encounter with romance ended when her boyfriend fled the country with *America's Most Wanted* hot on his heels. That kind of thing has a tendency to make a girl skittish.

But despite all the obstacles, love is in the air—boy, is it ever. And of course, there's always a happy ending. So please join Marci and Johnny on their trip across Texas, and let me know what you think of my slightly seasoned (aka Baby Boomer) hero and heroine.

Ann DeFee

Somewhere Down in Texas

ANN DeFee

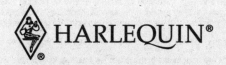

HARLEQUIN®

TORONTO • NEW YORK • LONDON
AMSTERDAM • PARIS • SYDNEY • HAMBURG
STOCKHOLM • ATHENS • TOKYO • MILAN • MADRID
PRAGUE • WARSAW • BUDAPEST • AUCKLAND

To Edie King—the world's best sister
and keeper of all my secrets.
Here's to our wonderful psychic connection.

ISBN-13: 978-0-373-75159-4
ISBN-10:   0-373-75159-1

SOMEWHERE DOWN IN TEXAS

Copyright © 2007 by Ann DeFee.

This edition published by arrangement with Harlequin Books S.A.

www.eHarlequin.com

Printed in U.S.A.

ABOUT THE AUTHOR

Ann DeFee's debut novel, *A Texas State of Mind* (Harlequin American Romance) was a double finalist in the 2006 Romance Writers' of America's prestigious RITA® Awards. Ann writes for both the Harlequin American Romance and Harlequin Everlasting lines. Look for upcoming books.

Drawing on her background as a fifth-generation Texan, Ann loves to take her readers into the sassy and sometimes wacky world of a small Southern community. As an air force wife with twenty-three moves under her belt, she's now settled in her tree house in the Pacific Northwest with her husband, their golden retriever and two very spoiled cats. When she's not writing, you can probably find her on the tennis court or in the park with her walking group.

She loves to hear from her readers, so please visit her Web site at www.ann-defee.com. Or contact her by snail mail at P.O. Box 97313, Tacoma, WA 98497.

Books by Ann DeFee

HARLEQUIN AMERICAN ROMANCE
1076—A TEXAS STATE OF MIND
1115—TEXAS BORN

DEFEE BARBECUE AND BASTING SAUCE

2 cloves garlic, crushed
1/2 cup ketchup
3/4 cup chili sauce
2 tbsp prepared mustard
1/2 tsp salt

2 tbsp butter, melted
3/4 cup water
1/4 cup brown sugar, packed
2 tbsp Worcestershire sauce
2 dashes hot sauce

1 tsp liquid smoke (mesquite)

Sauté garlic in butter, add ketchup and remaining ingredients; bring to a boil. Use to baste pork, chicken or beef during cooking. Yield: 3 cups.

Chapter One

"I have the most *fantastic* idea!" Sissy Aguirre announced as she sashayed into her sister's kitchen.

Uh-oh! Marci Hamilton resisted the urge to cross herself or wave a clove of garlic in the air for protection. When the words *fantastic* and *idea* appeared simultaneously in one of Sissy's sentences, it meant trouble.

Marci loved her sister, really she did, but sometimes the woman was a disaster waiting to happen. So in the interest of self-preservation, she silently continued to fix supper.

Exercising her right as firstborn, Sissy grabbed the potato Marci was peeling. "Stop that."

"Stop what?"

"Stop ignoring me. You know it makes me crazy. And don't you *dare* say what you're thinking."

The sisters had this annoying mind-reading skill they called their psychic episodes. Some people would call it second sight. Whatever it was, Marci knew when to pick her battles and when to concede gracefully, not that she'd ever agree to one of Sissy's wild ideas. Yeah, right.

"Okay, what is it?" Marci asked in an attempt to be polite.

In response, Sissy pulled a bottle of chilled Chardonnay from the refrigerator and held it up. "Wine?"

Good Lord! If this harebrained scheme required alcohol it had to be a doozy. "Sure." More than likely she'd need it.

"Harvey and I have come up with a great way to make money and we want you to help us."

On that note Marci marched to the cabinet and exchanged her wineglass for a large tumbler. "Fill 'er up," she demanded.

Although Harvey Johnson and Sissy had been divorced for almost twenty years, they were inseparable. They even bickered like an old married couple. He supposedly lived in Houston; however, for the past five years he'd spent most of his time at Sissy's house in the Texas gulf coast community of Port Serenity.

"Before we get into the details of this current plan, I have a question. Why *did* you two get divorced?" They were perfectly suited and obviously loved each other, so why *had* they called it quits?

Sissy stared at the golden liquid in her glass as if it held the secrets of the universe. The woman was stalling—highly unusual, since Sissy was never at a loss for words, or actions, for that matter.

"He put a ton of money into De Lorean."

"What in the *world* is a De Lorean?"

"It's a sports car some dude came up with in the eighties. They built about three hundred of them and then the company went belly up."

Of all the transgressions Marci expected her to reveal, that wasn't even on the radar screen. "Are you telling me that Harvey, our CPA Harvey, put money into an experimental car?"

Would wonders never cease!

Sissy nodded in agreement. "And that's not the worst of it. The final straw was when he invested in a wildcat oil well. Can you believe it?" She shook her head. "Talk about throwing good money after bad."

Harvey was about as fiscally conservative as Alan Greenspan. Still…

"You're telling me you divorced a man because of the way he invested?"

Although she and Sissy looked enough alike to be twins, Marci periodically had to wonder whether they really *had* come from the same gene pool.

"You got it."

"Did he make *some* profitable decisions?"

"Absolutely, he made money when other people were losing their shirts."

"So what was the problem?"

"The problem was I told him not to go with those stupid deals, and he did anyway."

"You are the biggest fruitcake on the face of the earth."

Wouldn't you know it—the insult didn't bother Sissy. They'd been sisters for sixty-odd years and Marci had never seen her back down from a decision. It was a darned good thing she was delightful, charming and zany because she was incredibly stubborn.

But back to the subject at hand. As much as Marci didn't want to do it, she had to get the details on the latest ditzy plan. Maybe, just maybe, she could waylay the insanity. Although the chances of that were probably slim to none—and everyone was familiar with what had happened to "slim."

"Okay, spill it."

Before Sissy could utter a word, the screen door flew open with a bang and a little blond whirlwind danced in.

"Hi, Mee Maw. Hi, Aunt Sissy." Marci's thirteen-year-old granddaughter, Amanda Delacroix, gave everyone a hug, then went straight for the cookie jar.

"Mama's putting the babies in the stroller. She'll be here in just a second," she said around a mouthful of chocolate. The mama in question was Lolly Delacroix—wife, mother and Port Serenity's police chief. The babies were Amanda's half sisters, Dana and Renée.

Sissy put her arm around the young girl's shoulders. "Swear to goodness, child, you're getting prettier every day. You're the spitting image of your mother, isn't she, Marcela?"

As she spoke, Lolly struggled through the door with a tandem stroller.

"Hi, Mom. Hi, Aunt Sissy," Lolly said as she maneuvered the unwieldy baby buggy around the table.

"How are my snookums doing?" Marci lapsed into baby talk as she leaned over to kiss each infant.

"And to answer your question, Sissy, she's definitely pretty as a picture. All my grandbabies are beautiful, even Bren," Marci said as she tugged her granddaughter into her lap. "And don't tell Bren I said that," she whispered to Amanda. Bren was Lolly's seventeen-year-old son—a high-school super jock—and well past the "I want to kiss Mee Maw" stage.

"Yeah, he wouldn't like it," Amanda agreed with a giggle.

But it was true. The entire clan was blessed with the same Nordic good looks—platinum hair, cornflower-blue eyes and the height of their long-ago Viking ancestors.

"Something smells delicious," Lolly commented as

she lifted the lid of the frying pan. "Smothered pork chops. I love smothered pork chops." Then she opened the oven door. "And corn bread. Gosh, my mouth's already watering. Thanks for inviting us to supper."

"Domino's is on our speed dial, you know," Amanda said. "When Daddy has a night meeting or Mama's tired, we have pizza."

"Really?" Marci asked, and Lolly responded with a shrug.

"Sometimes it feels like I'm chasing my tail, I'm so busy, and pizza contains all the major food groups. I haven't heard any complaints from Bren or Amanda, and these two—" Lolly indicated the twins "—don't have an opinion, yet. Not that they eat anything solid."

"What's Christian doing tonight?" Marci asked as she set the table.

Rénee started to fuss, so Lolly took the baby out of the stroller and handed her to Sissy. "They're working on a big case in the Rio Grande Valley. I hope it's finally coming to an end."

As the district director for the Texas Highway Patrol Narcotics Services, Christian was responsible for drug busts all over South Texas—and with the growing number of drug smugglers, pot growers and crystal meth cookers, he was a busy man.

"How's it working out with the day care at the station?" Marci asked. On one level, she missed baby-sitting the twins. On another, she was ecstatic. The full-time kid detail was exhausting.

"Ella Burbank is our head nanny now. She's Poochie Burbank's wife. You remember Poochie from when I was in high school, don't you?" Lolly asked her mother. "He's the one who toilet papered the principal's house and had to mow Mr. Granger's lawn for an entire spring and summer."

Sissy was bouncing the baby. "She's in my book club. I didn't realize she was doing child care."

"Yes, thank goodness. She's great with kids." Lolly turned to her mother. "Mama, is there anything I can do to help?"

Marci handed her the plates and utensils.

"We were lucky to get her. Now I don't feel so guilty when I have to work." Lolly sighed and continued to set the table. "Even though I have a great situation, being a working mom is tough."

The town council had allowed Lolly to create a mini-nursery at the police station, and Renée and Dana were now the darlings of the department. Lolly was thinking about haranguing them to fund an enlarged version of the nursery, so more employees could take advantage of it.

"Supper's served," Marci announced as she dished up the mashed potatoes. The scrumptious smell of home cooking wafted through the kitchen.

For a few minutes everyone ate silently while they savored the delicious meal, then Lolly introduced a new topic. "Aunt Sissy, I love your new do."

"Do you really?" Sissy ran her fingers through her spiked red hair. "For a second I was afraid it was too young-looking. Now I love it. I tried to get 'Miss Chicken'—" she pointed at Marci "—to go with a color but she claims blondes have more fun. We'll see about that."

"I want to get some of those cool streaks," Amanda said, picking up strands of her blond hair for a better view. "I'm not sure if I want purple or blue. What do you think?" She addressed her question to Sissy—smart girl—although her mother answered.

"I think *no.*"

"Mo-o-o-om!" She'd mastered the teenage ability to turn a monosyllabic word into a polysyllabic whine.

Lolly wasn't buying the pubescent angst. "We'll talk about it when you get into high school."

Without missing a beat Sissy changed the topic. "I was about to tell Marci about an idea that's pee-in-your-pants exciting."

Amanda giggled in response to the middle-school potty humor while Marci suppressed a groan.

Oh, dear! Sissy was so persuasive that once she aired her proposal, the entire family would jump on the bandwagon.

"What?" Amanda was always ready to try anything billed as new and exciting.

"You've all heard of J. W. Watson." Sissy paused until they nodded in unison. J. W. Watson was South Texas's contribution to the Country Music Hall of Fame. Anyone who'd ever done the Texas two-step was familiar with his songs.

"He has a new company that makes products like barbecue sauce and picante. J.W.'s doing the Paul Newman thing." Sissy fanned her face. "Paul Newman has the most gorgeous eyes I've ever seen. And J. W. Watson is pretty darned handsome, too. Not that you can really tell what he looks like. He has that mysterious thing going, but he is sexy as all heck. Don't you think, Marci?"

"Can't say I have an opinion. Andrea Bocelli is more my speed." Her comment obviously fell on deaf ears because Sissy kept yammering. It was tempting to interrupt her segue from picante sauce to sexy men, but when you were dealing with Sissy, patience was a virtue. Or, more to the point, a necessity. Eventually she'd get back on track.

"Anyway, he's sponsoring a series of barbecue sauce cook-offs. And he's offering big money for the best recipe. Really big money!" she exclaimed.

Marci could tell where this was going. Their mother's sauce had won multiple blue ribbons at the county fair.

"I submitted Mama's recipe in the preliminary contest and our team's one of the twenty finalists." Sissy jumped up and plucked her purse from the counter. "It's official!" She waved a piece of paper in the air. "Nashville Network, here we come. TV—can you imagine it? *We're* gonna be on TV." Sissy was positively beaming as she shared her good news.

"TV?" Amanda joined in on the excitement. "That's way cool. Don't you think so, Mee Maw? I can't wait to tell Leslie." Leslie was her best friend and the keeper of all her secrets.

Marci could see that Lolly was trying to suppress a bout of giggles. Merciful heavens. What had Sissy gotten them into *this* time?

"I hate to encourage you, but why don't you share the details? And don't gloat because I haven't agreed to anything," Marci said. Not that she had a chance against her steamroller sibling. Unfortunately, Sissy was aware of that particular weakness.

"Here's the deal." Sissy did a little tap dance across the linoleum. "The cook-offs will feature teams of contestants." She stopped dancing long enough to throw Marci a smirk. "One of which will be you and me. And Harv has volunteered to man the barbecue pit, even though he won't be an official team member. Isn't he a sweet man? Anyway, they're holding these culinary escapades at dance halls and rodeos all over Texas. The TV folks will be there, front and center. The first week we go to Gruene, and the next week we head off to Luckenbach. The third weekend we all move to the Ozona rodeo and the last event's at the Festival of Lights in Marfa." She did another pirouette. "Doesn't that sound like *fun?*"

Not really.

"Think money, lots of money. You could buy that VW convertible you've been wanting." Sissy waved the acceptance notice under Marci's nose. "The teams accrue points at each contest, and when all's said and done, the guys and/or girls with the most points win. At the end of the day, I'm planning to walk off with that man's hundred thousand dollars."

Sissy certainly didn't need the money, so Marci suspected her motivation leaned more toward the thrill of being on TV.

Television. Yikes!

Chapter Two

"Marci," Sissy chirped. "I have something terrific to show you." She whirled into Marci's living room the next afternoon, with Harvey following in her wake. "You're absolutely not going to believe it. I am *so* excited."

Actually, Marci was having a hard time believing she'd agreed to the barbecue idea in the first place. Especially after she discovered that Harvey was going to haul a "portable barbecue pit" (a fifty-five-gallon drum cut in half with wheels on it) halfway across Texas. Talk about looking like the Clampetts. What had happened to cute little aprons, stainless steel stoves and health department inspections?

"Come outside with me." Sissy grabbed Marci's hand and pulled her to the front door of the townhouse.

"Check it out!" She pointed at the brand-new cherry red T-Bird convertible in the driveway. "I made Harv go with me to the dealer this morning. Isn't it about the sexiest set of wheels you've ever seen?"

Marci reluctantly admitted Sissy was right. And darn it, she'd always been a sucker for hot cars.

"It's absolutely perfect for our adventure. Remember after your college graduation when we took a road trip to sample margaritas all over the country? And we met those guys in Taos and—"

"Of course I remember," Marci interrupted. That was the trip of a lifetime, and heaven help her if Sissy wanted to replicate it. Sometimes Sissy conveniently blanked out the fact that they were both *grandmothers*.

Marci wandered out to admire the soft leather seats and the five-speed stick shift. Wind in her hair, Michael Bolton on the CD—it had possibilities. She ran her hand across the shiny hood. It sure beat the heck out of her serviceable, but uninspiring, Honda.

"You've sold me."

"Atta girl." Sissy tossed the keys to her sister. "Put your butt in the driver's seat. We're going shoppin'." She jumped in to ride shotgun. "Every woman can use some retail therapy."

Harvey leaned in to plant a big kiss on Sissy's lips. "You girls be careful now, ya hear."

Marci glanced at the couple now fully engaged in a lip lock. They were obviously in love, so why did they get divorced in the first place? Oh, right—it was all about a De Lorean. How stupid was that?

"Hate to break this up." Naw, she didn't really. Marci turned the ignition, and the powerful engine growled to life. She popped it into first gear and off they shot, almost before Harvey had a chance to retrieve his lips.

Michael was crooning on the CD, the wind was fluffing her platinum-blond pageboy and Marci was feeling young and sexy. As much as she hated to admit it, this might be one of Sissy's better ideas.

"Do you have a game plan for our shopping spree?" Marci had to yell to be heard over the music and wind noise.

"Yep, head to Robstown," Sissy answered.

"Robstown?" Robstown was a farming community that was the home to the Robstown High School Cotton Pickers, Cotton-Eyed Joe's Dance Emporium and the Pit Restaurant (famous throughout South Texas for its barbecue).

"Mrs. Pomerantz told me that Carter's Farm and Ranch Supply has the best selection of cowboy boots around. I can't imagine how she became an expert on kicker boots, but swear to goodness, that woman knows everything."

Mrs. Pomerantz was an icon in Port Serenity. She was in her seventies or eighties, it was hard to tell, and somehow she always managed to be in the middle of the action. Once she almost single-handedly started a riot on Main Street. And then there was the time she found the bodies in the wildlife refuge.

Why *wouldn't* she be a fashion maven?

"Okay. If we can't find anything there, we can always check Penney's in the mall," Marci agreed.

"Penney's! Are you kidding me?" Sissy wiggled her booty. "*We're* going to be on TV! We have to be the divas of western fashion."

MARCI WAS ASTONISHED that she'd never noticed Carter's. It was gigantic. The outside display area featured tractors (who knew they came in that many sizes and shapes), corral fencing, horse trailers (a family of four could take up residence in one of those puppies) and mundane items like stock troughs and rolls of barbed wire. The outside of the building was impressive; however, it was nothing compared to the inside of the store.

"It looks like the clothes and boots are in the back,"

Sissy proclaimed as they walked past a line of saddles inlaid with silver and a display of turquoise cowboy hats.

"Too bad Roy and Dale aren't around. They'd have loved this," Marci commented as she fingered one of the elaborate saddles. She almost swooned when she picked up the price tag and discovered it cost as much as her car. Penney's was looking more and more appealing.

"We'll start with the boots and work our way back toward the register. By the time we're finished, we'll be so western Clint Eastwood's gonna be envious."

Marci thought that was a stretch, but before she could object, Sissy flipped her shoes off and summoned a clerk.

And that signaled Marci's entry into the world of cowboy boots. The selection ran the gamut from Tony Lama full quill ostrich to Justin iguana lizard. Unfortunately, they were all mega-expensive.

It wasn't that Marci was poor; however, she did have to be frugal. Her husband, Trey, a Port Serenity police officer, was shot during a traffic stop when Lolly was a teenager. After that, they lived on his insurance and death benefits, plus her kindergarten teacher's salary.

Sissy, on the other hand, had money to burn. Three years after she divorced Harvey, she married Eduardo Aguirre, heir to a banana plantation in Central America. He was almost twenty years her senior, which didn't bother her; she was in love. The fact that he dropped dead on their honeymoon did distress her—a lot. The authorities said it was a heart attack. However, Sissy suspected he'd succumbed to a peanut allergy. Damn those cruise ship buffets.

That was Sissy's last foray into marriage; however, it didn't take Harvey more than a year to snuggle back into her life. And he'd been promoting his position in her affections ever since.

"The red hand-tooled ones are nice." Sissy held up one foot. "But the snakeskins make me feel exotic." She raised her other foot. "What do you think?"

What Marci thought was that they should find some boots that cost $39.95. They had to be dressed appropriately to be on TV, but three-hundred-dollar boots? No way!

"Actually, I'm partial to these." Marci held up a pair of black suede Tony Lamas with insets of red roses. "I can't afford them, darn it, so I guess I'll go with this pair." Her second choice was plain red Ropers. "Then I won't have to consult a loan officer to get out of here."

Sissy grabbed the black Tony Lamas and thrust them at the clerk. "We'll take these and the snakeskins." She linked arms with Marci. "I'll pay for them and you can reimburse me from our winnings."

"And now, we need some new duds." Sissy marched confidently toward the racks of blouses, skirts and jeans. It was a sea of color and variety—rhinestones and fringe, lace and denim, sexy and utilitarian.

Two hours later, the dressing room was a mess and the sisters had selected a pile of skirts, jeans and shirts. Sissy's taste ran more toward slinky, while Marci favored prairie skirts and Victorian lace blouses. Fortunately, they were the same size so they'd be able to share clothes.

"I've had shopping up to here." Marci made a slashing motion across her throat. "And I'm starved." Plus, she was getting a headache.

"Me, too." Sissy zipped her pants and scooped up a pile of clothing. "I'll give these to the clerk so she can figure out how much we owe."

That had the potential to really ramp up Marci's headache.

"Let's go to the Pit for barbecue. We can check out their sauce." Following her pronouncement, Sissy made a sweeping exit from the dressing room.

Marci had a feeling that before this was over, she'd be sick to death of barbecue. She also suspected this adventure would either be an unmitigated disaster or a life-changing event.

Unfortunately, she didn't have a clue which it would turn out to be.

Chapter Three

"How'd it go in Houston?"

Before J. W. "Johnny" Watson answered his business manager's question, he viciously yanked at the knot in his tie and sank down into the plush leather chair behind the mahogany desk.

"Damn it to hell!" Johnny slammed his fist on the polished surface. "It's been ten years since Marina and I divorced, and she can still send my blood pressure into the stratosphere. I can't believe she put her name on that piece-of-trash book. Novel, my butt. You know as well as I do that it's about me. My God, she can barely put together a cogent sentence, must less a whole book, so we know she used a ghost writer. And that's just one more person involved in this debacle." He let out a big huff and flopped back.

"Guess I should be glad I'm such a laid-back fella or I might have to hit something. Or someone." Johnny punctuated that remark with one of his trademark grins.

Brian quickly returned to the theme of the conversation. "And I guess it's a good thing we're best friends, 'cause I can tell you stuff no one else would dare say."

That was true. Brian Banfield was not only Johnny's

best friend, he was also his business manager and godfather to his son, Randy. And, nineteen years ago he'd
been the lone voice of caution when Johnny made the
biggest mistake of his life—marrying Marina.

"What did he say?" The "he" Brian was referring to
was Johnny's lawyer, Jason Scuggs.

Johnny rubbed a hand across his face. "He said that
because the work is fiction—" he made quote marks
in the air "—we can't stop her. No matter how bad it
makes me look."

Both men fell into the silence commonplace to a
long-term friendship. "I've always thought she was des-
picable, but I didn't have any idea she'd sink this far,"
Brian said.

"She can't be doing it for the money. I gave her a
truckload of cash in the divorce settlement." Johnny
wandered over to the bar to retrieve an unopened bottle
of Johnny Walker Blue Label and a Baccarat crystal
tumbler. "Want one?" Not waiting for an answer, he
splashed two fingers of amber gold in each glass and
handed one to his friend.

Brian took an appreciative sip before he spoke.
"When things are gettin' rough, you break out the expensive stuff." Brian grinned in an attempt to ease the
tension. "As for Marina's motivation, haven't you heard
the saying that you can't be too rich or too thin?"

That hit the nail on the head. The she-witch was
stick-thin, filthy rich and as mean as a prairie rattler. Just
the thought of his anorexic ex-wife gave Johnny a case
of heartburn. About two weeks after the wedding he
knew he'd made a huge mistake, but he didn't believe
in divorce so he'd tried his best to make the marriage
work. By the time he conceded it was a no-win situa-

tion, Marina had announced she was pregnant. And in a misguided attempt to create a family for his son, he spent many miserable years with the wrong person.

God, what a mess, Johnny thought as he ambled back to his favorite chair.

Brian hesitated a moment and then continued. "I think there's something worse motivating her. I suspect she's obsessed with you. If that's true, she'll be more dangerous than that chick in *Fatal Attraction*."

"Do you really think she's obsessed?"

"I'm afraid I do. Marina's mental health is unstable at best. That's why the judge gave you full custody of Randy and limited her to visitation rights on holidays. I do have to give her credit for realizing she wasn't capable of raising a child."

Johnny frowned. "She's a sick woman. I'm worried about how this will affect Randy. Being a teenager is tough. Having a famous father is even more difficult. And when you add Marina into the mix, you have a big problem."

"He's a bright kid," Brian said with confidence. "He knows you're nothing like the sleazeball in that book. As a matter of fact, you're the best dad around and he's well aware of it. He learned how to deal with Marina when he was a toddler."

Randall Xavier Watson III was Johnny's eighteen-year-old son. He was the only good thing to come out of that marriage.

"I sure hope so." Johnny shook his head in an attempt to dislodge his post-Scuggs headache. "After that piece of smut hits the bookstores, everyone in America's gonna figure I'm just a coke-snorting womanizer."

"Aren't you?" Brian emphasized his question with a

snort. That was just a touch of good-natured sarcasm since Johnny was known throughout the country-music scene as one of the good guys.

Leave it to Brian to introduce some levity to the situation. "Yeah, sure, and that's why I haven't had a date in two years." He grinned at his friend. "Taking your sister to the Country Music Awards last year doesn't count."

Their conversation was cut short when Randy appeared in the door. "Hey, Dad, the plane's in the hangar and I'm going in to town to meet some guys." Flying was Randy's passion, and he was crazy about Johnny's Gulfstream. He'd obtained his private pilot's license when he was only sixteen, and consequently he spent every spare minute exploring the wild blue yonder.

God, Johnny loved that kid. "Call if you're going to be late." His son was old enough to vote, and yes, in three months he'd be at Texas A&M, but Johnny couldn't resist playing daddy. For ten years it'd been the two of them against the world, so letting go was going to be *really* hard.

"Have a good time," Johnny called, even though Randy was already out the door.

"I'm heading home," Brian said. "Karin wants me to help her paint the kitchen."

"Don't I pay you enough to hire someone to do that?"

"And miss Karin's special reward for a little hard work? Not gonna happen," Brian replied with a smug smile.

And that, Johnny thought ruefully, was what he was missing—the love of a good woman.

AFTER BRIAN AND Randy left, Johnny sat and enjoyed the view from his office window. This was his little piece of South Texas heaven with its rolling green hills dotted with ancient live oak and mesquite trees. Everything else paled in importance to home and his son. Nashville was fine on a temporary basis, but this was where he belonged. It was his reality.

The original hacienda was over a hundred and fifty years old. In the time since Johnny bought the ranch he'd done an extensive remodel and added a new wing; however, he'd retained the historical integrity of the house. Bella Vista was a showplace featuring two-foot-thick adobe walls, an interior courtyard and priceless antiques from the Mexican colonial period. He'd also made sure it was a comfortable place where they could walk around barefoot and leave newspapers on the coffee table.

Johnny glanced out the window at the herd of white-faced Herefords grazing in the pasture and knew exactly what he needed to do. Mindless physical labor was the only thing that would get rid of the knots in his shoulders. And there wasn't anything more mindless and physical than riding fence and stringing barbed wire.

"MAMA, ARE YOU SURE you have everything? Sunglasses, cell phone, sunscreen…"

"Passport?" Jeeze, she might be in her sixties but she was too young for her daughter to be taking on parental duties.

"What would you need a passport for? You're just going to New Braunfels," Lolly said.

"Exactly." Marci gave her daughter a hug. "We have a cell phone, a reliable car and a hotel reservation. What more could we want?"

"I know, I know." Lolly fell into a chair. "It's just that

Aunt Sissy's project makes me nervous. I love her dearly, although I sometimes wonder about her sanity."

Sometimes Marci wondered, too; however, she wasn't about to back out now.

"I can't believe Uncle Harvey agreed to haul that—" Lolly waved her hand in the air "—barbecue-pit around South Texas behind his Suburban. The man's an accountant, for goodness' sake. Doesn't he have a lick of sense?"

"He's in love and that'll make a guy do some unusual stuff."

"What's with the kissy face? Why don't they get remarried?" Lolly asked.

Now that was the question of the century. Too bad Marci didn't have an answer.

Before the conversation could continue, Sissy strolled into the kitchen wearing a hot-pink Stetson with a silver hatband.

"Wow, that's eye-catching!" Lolly exclaimed.

Especially considering it clashed with Sissy's brilliant red hair.

"Cute. Tell me you're not planning to wear it on TV," Marci demanded.

Lolly simply rolled her eyes.

"I don't know if I am or not, but let's get going. We're supposed to be in New Braunfels by late afternoon. Harvey's bringing the equipment tomorrow." Sissy turned to her niece and grinned. "Did Marci tell you we have reservations at Victoria's Mansion? I am *so* excited! I've never stayed there because it's très expensive. But the TV people are paying, so I can pamper myself with a clear conscience."

"Since those rooms cost over two hundred dollars a

night it's a darned good thing the Nashville Network's footing the bill," Marci agreed.

"Are you ready?" Sissy slapped the Stetson against her thigh. "We have people to see and places to go. Chop, chop." She made a shooing motion with her hands.

"I'm ready. Keep your drawers on." Marci tugged on the handle of her bag and grabbed her sunglasses. "Let's roll."

THE SUN WAS SHINING, the humidity was low and the thermometer was barely over the eighty-degree mark. All in all, it was a great day for a convertible, an unusual occurrence for Texas in late June.

Plus, they had Willie and Waylon crooning about love at the truck stop, and a two-pound bag of M&M's within reach. What more could a couple of hip seniors need for an adventure? Oh, yeah, a map might be nice, particularly since they were irretrievably lost—on a gravel road, no less—in the middle of nowhere.

"I can't believe you didn't pack a map. Every car has a map. It's some kind of unwritten rule," Marci exclaimed. She was beyond exasperated and desperately trying to keep from stopping the car and smacking her sister. They'd been driving around for what seemed like hours, and so far they hadn't seen any sign of civilization. It was cows, cows and more cows. And every time Sissy gave her directions, they found themselves deeper in the labyrinth of farm-to-farm roads that criss-crossed Texas. To make matters worse, the low fuel light had come on several miles back.

"Don't get snotty with me. You're the one who got us lost in the first place." Sissy pushed her sunglasses up higher on her nose and put on her pouty face.

Good Lord, she could be muleheaded. Marci took a deep breath, and then another. Deep breathing was good. She had a great comeback, but suspected it wouldn't be wise to use it. The only reason she was at the wheel was Sissy thought I-37 was the Indianapolis Speedway, and the cute highway patrolman had expressed some serious objections about her driving ability.

Focus. Focus. Focus. They were somewhere between Beeville and Seguin—and only God knew their exact location. So considering that Marci was directionally impaired and couldn't read a map even if they had one, they were in a boatload of trouble.

She could see it now. Lolly would have them on some kind of Lost and Presumed Abducted list before the sun set.

If in doubt, grab an M&M. "Okay, let's look at this logically. If we turn around and follow the road back the way we came, we'll eventually get to some pavement. And pavement will eventually mean a sign, and a sign will lead us to civilization. That is, if we have enough gas."

"And hopefully a Dairy Queen because I'm starving," Sissy muttered.

Marci threw the bag of candy into her sister's lap. The woman was as bad as a kid.

"Look at that." Sissy squealed and pointed down the road.

"What am I looking for?" Marci squinted in the direction her sister was pointing.

"See that horse? Well, there's a man standing right next to it. I'm sure he can tell us how to get back to town."

Since they were in the middle of the frickin' backwoods, that might be a leap of faith—but hey, they were out of options. And, yes, in the far, far distance Marci could barely make out the silhouette of a man.

"Let's hope we haven't found the local rapist," she murmured as she put the T-Bird in gear. "I suppose you forgot the pepper spray, too."

Sissy stuck out her tongue.

JOHNNY HAD finished patching a section of barbed wire when a red T-Bird wheeled to a stop. He lived in the boon-docks for a reason—his desire for privacy. If they were paparazzi, they were about to get a piece of his mind.

Then he took a good look and liked what he saw. The two women weren't youngsters, but neither was he. The young groupies who flocked to his concerts hadn't jump-started his libido since he was twenty-five, and that'd been a few decades back.

Although the redhead was a bit much, the blonde was a classy-looking lady. He was about to clamber over the fence and see what they needed when he noticed they were having an argument. Every time the redhead started to talk, the blonde shook her head. Finally the blonde got out of the car and slammed the door so hard the vehicle rocked.

That one had a temper. Interesting.

As she stomped closer, he could see she was beauti-ful—tall and willowy, with shoulder-length platinum hair bordering on silver, and the prettiest blue eyes he'd ever seen. And, if her expression was any indication, she was in a royal snit.

"Howdy, ma'am. Can I help you?" He pulled his Stetson further over his eyes. The last thing he wanted to deal with was an ardent fan.

She huffed out a big breath. "We're lost and it's my

sister's fault," she muttered. "I'm Marci Hamilton and that's my sister, Sissy." She pointed at the redhead then stuck out her hand.

Since Johnny had been riding fence he was dirty and sweaty, but he didn't want to embarrass her, so he wiped his hand on his jeans before extending it.

At the last minute he decided to go with his middle name. "I'm Johnny Walker."

"Johnny Walker?"

He could tell she was on the verge of laughing, and for some unknown reason that fascinated him.

"My daddy had a good sense of humor," Johnny said.

"Well, Johnny Walker, could you tell us how to get to town? Any town will do, although one with a Dairy Queen would be nice."

"Yes, ma'am, I can sure do that. In fact, I can do you one better. If you ladies will stay here, I'll ride back and get my pickup. Then you can follow me into Live Oak."

Instinctively he realized she was unsure about his invitation, so he resisted the grin he felt coming on. Johnny also refused to acknowledge his racing pulse and clammy hands. Was he having a heart attack or had he fallen in sudden lust with a total stranger? It'd been so long since he'd felt anything even vaguely similar, he wasn't sure what was going on.

Whatever it was, this woman was enticing and he hadn't been tempted by a woman in years. And best of all, she didn't recognize him.

Hot damn! Maybe it was his lucky day.

Chapter Four

"He's going back to get his pickup and lead us into town."

"Back where?" Sissy asked, shading her eyes, looking for a ranch house or a bar or something.

"What am I? A mind-reader? He probably has a double-wide out in those trees," Marci responded. Sister dearest was already getting on her nerves, and they'd just started their trip. "I wish I'd asked him to bring some extra fuel. Sometimes these ranches have their own gas pumps." She paused. "What if he's dangerous?"

"You worry too much, ya know that?" Sissy flipped a hand in apparent dismissal of Marci's concerns. She took out a tube of lip gloss and a compact. "Never hurts to appear your best," Sissy said as she fluffed her hair. "Did you check out that body of his? He was just sweaty enough for a nice sheen. There's something about a guy engaged in physical labor that gives me the chills."

Marci resisted the urge to knock some sense into her. Now was not the time to get the hots for some *cowboy*, regardless of how sweaty he was. Twenty minutes later, she was beginning to wonder whether the sexy cowboy really would return.

And he *was* sexy, in a rugged Texas way. Not that she

could tell much about his looks with that hat pulled down around his eyes. But his voice, a deep black-velvet drawl, was enough to make a female melt into a puddle of rampant hormones.

When perspiration began to drip down her cleavage, Marci decided she had to have some shade. "I'm hot, so I'm going to put up the top."

"Party pooper," Sissy commented as she threw another handful of M&M's into her mouth.

Marci suspected that Miss Priss was also about to expire from the heat but was too stubborn to admit it.

"There he is." Sissy pointed at the cloud of dust that was rapidly approaching.

Salvation in the form of a battered Ford F-150 pickup was on the horizon.

"Thank goodness." Marci's heartfelt sense of relief quickly dissipated when she studied their new friend as he uncurled long legs from the cab of a truck that was well past the salvage-yard stage.

With his scuffed boots, faded jeans, sunglasses and battered hat he looked like he'd stepped out of a spaghetti western—and he wasn't playing the role of the hero.

"I'm not so sure about this," Marci muttered.

Sissy replied with a snort. "We don't have a choice. In case you haven't noticed, we're lost."

No kidding. And if they ran out of gas they'd be totally at his mercy.

Talk about a portent of things to come.

As they passed the first road sign they'd seen in miles, and Marci could virtually smell civilization, the T-Bird coughed a couple of times and died. Right there on that gravel road, the pride of Detroit gave up the ghost. Aarrggh!

"Where's the pepper spray?" Marci mumbled as the man named Johnny stopped his truck and ambled toward the car.

"I didn't get any." Sissy was wearing her guilty face. "The place was closed when I went by, and then I got so busy I forgot."

"What?" Marci resisted the urge to beat her head on the steering wheel. Could they jump out of a moving truck and live? She hoped to God she wasn't about to find out.

"Is there a problem, ladies?" he asked.

Marci hesitated a moment, and then spilled the beans. "We're out of gas."

He made a noise that started out sounding like a chuckle and ended in a cough. "Really? Looks like you're gonna have to ride into town with me to get a gas can."

"Couldn't you leave us here and bring some back? I'll pay you," Marci said.

He did that funny chuckle/cough thing again. "Well, ma'am, I don't think so. I wouldn't feel right deserting you. You're perfectly safe with me, I promise." He opened the car door and held out a hand to assist her. Okay, the man had manners, but that didn't mean he wasn't a serial killer.

Reluctantly she followed him to the pickup. Sissy, the dork, was acting like this was all a big game. Didn't she watch *Court TV*?

The interior of the pickup was almost worse than the exterior. Marci could ignore the tufts of padding that peeked out of the cracked vinyl seats, but the fact that the door handle was missing sent chills up her spine. That would make a quick exit rather difficult.

"Are you positive I can't pay you for your time and gas?" she asked. The guy was obviously as poor as a church mouse and he was going out of his way to help them.

"No, ma'am, I wouldn't hear of it," he responded with a grin.

JOHNNY CHUCKLED to himself. Marci was as skittish as a newborn filly, and why not—their current transportation was the ranch's oldest utility vehicle. The cowboys had hauled everything from horse manure to tractor parts in it. And from the smell, Johnny had to assume some barnyard animal had recently spent time in the front seat. He'd have to ask his foreman.

The good news was that neither lady seemed to recognize him, even now, despite getting a close-up and personal look. Considering his fame, that was kind of hard to believe, so he decided to do a little test. He turned on the radio—at least it worked—and quickly found a station playing a selection of Martina McBride songs.

"You ladies like country western music?" he asked, hoping to achieve a nonchalant tone.

"I've heard of George Strait, Waylon Jennings and J. W. Watson," Sissy piped up, "not that I'm a big fan or anything. I'm more into R & B." Marci didn't utter a word.

"How about you?" He addressed his question to her.

"I don't think I'd recognize any of them, but I've heard of the ones Sissy mentioned. Plus, I know about Willie Nelson. Anything beyond that and I'm pretty clueless."

Good answer.

MARCI'S FIRST SIGHT of civilization was the Dairy Queen sign. Praise the Lord! Any place that had a Dairy Queen would have a gas station and a telephone, and more than likely they'd also have a sheriff's deputy.

"Do you mind if we whip into the DQ and get a cold drink? I'm parched." Marci hated asking him to give up more work time and she wouldn't have made the request if her mouth wasn't completely dry. Worrying about serial killers tended to have that effect.

"Sure enough. I was going to suggest we stop for coffee," Johnny agreed as he turned into the crowded parking lot.

Marci felt like an idiot for being worried, but someone had to do it and Sissy didn't believe in anxiety. She claimed it gave her wrinkles. The hell with wrinkles. But Marci was *almost* positive this guy was harmless. Still, it wouldn't hurt to drop a few hints, just on the off chance they went missing.

"Hi, Johnny. You want the regular?" The girl at the counter popped her gum in rhythm to a Patsy Cline tune that even Marci recognized.

"Yep, and I'm picking up these ladies' tab."

Marci opened her mouth to protest but immediately snapped it shut, realizing the futility of that action. She'd known the man all of what—twenty minutes—and she already knew a couple of things about him. One, he was a gentleman right down to the tips of his boots, and a Texas gent always paid. And two, when he decided to do something, he did it his way. Stubborn was a trait she was *very* familiar with.

Sissy studied the overhead menu and finally decided on a Butterfinger Blizzard. "I'm headin' to the little girls' room. Grab my order when it comes up, okay?"

Sissy was gone before Marci had a chance to utter a word. Their male companion was standing at the counter watching her.

"I'll take a small hot fudge sundae and a large water,

please." She thought for a few seconds and figured that a bit of safety was worth looking like a lunatic. The woman's name tag indicated her name was Shari. "Shari, we ran out of gas and this gentleman picked us up in his truck. That truck." Marci pointed at the vehicle parked in front of the plate glass window. "The rusted blue one. My sister and I are from Port Serenity. That's down on the coast, you know." Marci was about to continue, but then she noticed the look on Shari's face. Her mouth hung open as she glanced from Johnny to Marci and then back to Johnny. He responded with that now familiar half chuckle and cough.

"Whatever." Marci waved a hand in the air. "Just remember it's the rusted blue truck." She made one last effort to convey her message. "And we have a red T-Bird convertible. Remember, it's a red T-Bird." Marci turned to Johnny. "You need to take care of that cough."

"Yes, ma'am. I'll sure do that." His concession was accompanied by the most charming lopsided grin Marci had ever seen.

"Johnny, here's your strawberry shake." Shari handed him his cup of ice cream. However, she set Marci's sundae and Sissy's Blizzard on the counter and stepped away a few feet. "Y'all come back now, ya hear?" she said before she scooted off.

"I think you scared her."

"Scared her? What did I do?"

He chuckled and slid a hand under Marci's elbow as he led her to a booth.

In true Texas fashion he removed his hat, providing Marci with her first good look at the mystery man. She'd already determined that he was tall and broad-shouldered. What she hadn't noticed was that he was one of those guys who aged like a fine wine. It didn't take a second glance to realize he was a potent combination of distinguished and sexy. And the distinguished part came as a huge surprise.

He was also much older than she'd thought, probably well into his fifties. His sable-brown hair was liberally sprinkled with silver and it curled around his collar. And he had the most sensual lips Marci had ever seen. Too bad they were framed by one of those droopy mustaches that looked like it belonged in a Billy the Kid western.

Marci was wondering why he was still wearing his sunglasses when Sissy returned.

"Hubba, hubba," her sister whispered. "Do you like being a cowboy?" she asked in a louder voice.

"Yes, ma'am, Miss Sissy, I do like being outdoors," he answered. However, he didn't elaborate. "And what are you ladies doing wandering around Texas?"

His question was enough to get Sissy started. "We're going to New Braunfels. We're finalists in a barbecue sauce contest. The first cook-off is next Saturday in Gruene."

Leave it to Sissy to be the mistress of too much information.

"It's sponsored by J. W. Watson. You know? The singer," she continued. "We're gonna be on television. Isn't that exciting?"

"It sure is, ma'am," Johnny said. More than they could imagine.

"Maybe you could come to Gruene to watch us cook." Sissy issued an invitation.

"Maybe I could," he agreed. "Maybe I could do just that."

Chapter Five

When Johnny discovered the sisters were contestants in *his* contest, he had the craziest desire to click his heels together.

It was fate at its finest.

Almost before they drove off—with a map and specific directions to the interstate—Johnny was on the phone to his business manager explaining the situation. He intended to tour the barbecue circuit. His big problem would be to keep his identity secret. Maintaining anonymity in Live Oak was easy; they were used to J. W. Watson sightings. Anyplace else could be a big problem.

"You won't be able to do this," Brian observed. "You're a celebrity. Tons of people recognize you."

"They see what they want to see. I'm thinking a short haircut, a baseball cap, a shave, shirts with little animals on the pocket and sunglasses. Your job is to call everyone we know and pepper them with bribes and threats."

Brian laughed so hard he reached the hiccup stage. "Gotcha. We might—hic—be able to make it work in—hic—Gruene. Luckenbach is gonna be another—hic—story."

Luckenbach was the site of the rustic dance hall that

was the hub of Texas country music. Anyone who was anyone would show up at a J. W. Watson–sponsored event in Luckenbach.

"Luckenbach will be tough. So we'll have to work around it." Johnny paused, waiting to see if his friend would come up with a brilliant idea.

"I need to—hic—think about this one."

That wasn't exactly the answer Johnny expected. So he tried to explain why this was so important to him.

"It's true that I just met her, but for some reason I think she's special." He refused to discuss, even with his best friend, his inexplicable attack of desire. "And I want to get to know her without all the garbage associated with fame."

There was a pause on the other end of the line. "I'll be at the ranch in—hic—twenty minutes. We'll figure it out."

TO PROVIDE ENTERTAINMENT during the competition, Johnny had hired his old buddy Vince McDowell and his band. Vince didn't know it yet, but he was about to provide the perfect cover for Johnny's ruse. J. W. Watson, superstar, was going to morph into Johnny Walker, roadie. Getting his old buddy on board wouldn't be that difficult, especially considering their history. It took a few tries, but Johnny finally managed to catch him on his cell phone.

"Hey, Vince, what's happenin'?"

"Nope, I won't do it."

"What makes you think I want a favor?"

"Because I've known you for over thirty years and I have a foolproof radar for panhandlers and scammers. Which is it?"

Johnny chuckled at Vince's observation. "I guess

you'd call it a scam." He proceeded to fill in his old friend on what he wanted to accomplish.

"Why don't you pick up some thirty-something with big hooters and call it good."

"Nope. That sounds—" Johnny paused as he tried to find the right word "—incestuous. Not that I have any daughters or anything, but it doesn't float my boat."

"Hey, everyone to his own thing," Vince said with a sigh. "Tell me what you want me to do."

Johnny knew he could count on Vince. Although he might be crusty, cranky and sometimes downright profane, he was one of Johnny's closest friends. He also happened to be the granddaddy of Texas country music. People came from far and wide to hear him.

During his drinking days, Vince had been a frequent guest of the Nashville cops, and consequently, Johnny was on a first-name basis with a local bail bondsman. Vince owed him, big time, and Johnny intended to collect. What better place to play "hide the country star" than in plain sight.

Since he was about to become part of Vince McDowell's entourage, there were plans to be made, a disguise to be created and favors to be called in. The handlebar mustache was his trademark, so that was the first that had to go. Ditto for the Stetson. Darn it!

THE FIRST FESTIVAL was slated to be held in Gruene— pronounced green—a picturesque village on the Guadalupe River. Anyone who envisioned Texas as a land of plains and sagebrush had never been to Gruene. Nestled in a fertile valley, Gruene was settled in the middle part of the nineteenth century by German immigrant farmers.

Originally the economic center of a 6,000-acre cotton plantation, the small community had endured a series of financial downturns until the 1970s, when there was nothing remaining but a run-down dance hall, a general store, a defunct cotton mill and an aging Victorian mansion.

During the Age of Aquarius, some far-sighted entrepreneurs revived the Gruene Dance Hall and enticed a group of up-and-coming country singers to do weekly gigs. Not only did their business decision help launch the careers of such stars as Willie Nelson, George Strait, Lyle Lovett, Jerry Jeff Walker and Kinky Friedman, it also heralded the upsurge of the Gruene community.

So now Gruene was all gussied up as it opened its arms to visitors from far and near. Whether they came for a day's outing or a week, they could indulge in Texas dining at the Grist Mill, shop at numerous antique stores and boutiques, or polish their boots for some two-steppin' at the oldest dance emporium in Texas. For more adventurous souls, the Guadalupe River was the perfect place for inner tubing, rafting, swimming and sunbathing. It was Texas fun at its very best.

"I'LL ADMIT IT," Marci said as she surveyed their two-bedroom guest cottage with its weathered clapboard siding and tin roof. "This is great. The outside is primitive but the interior is gorgeous."

"Not that I like to gloat, but I told you so."

Who was she kidding? Sissy had perfected gloating while she was still in diapers, so Marci simply ignored her.

"What do we do now?"

"I'm going to unpack," Sissy announced, wheeling a huge suitcase into her bedroom.

She'd brought enough clothes for a six-month journey. Not that it was any of Marci's business—unless big sis tried to hog all the hangers. Then all bets were off.

"I suggest we have dinner and then walk around town. I'd like to check out the venue for the cook-off," Sissy said as she strolled into Marci's room and grabbed a handful of hangers.

"Don't take them all," Marci commanded, even though she knew she was spitting in the wind.

Marci was having big misgivings about this whole cook-off venture. What if they gave someone food poisoning? On second thought, there'd be more health department inspectors than ants on a birthday cake, so that probably wouldn't happen. Before Marci could conjure up another apocalyptic scenario, Sissy tossed in one of her conversational bombs.

"Remember we have a TV briefing in the morning. They want to check out our clothes to make sure they film okay." Sissy did a pirouette holding a bright red fringed shirt to her bosom. "Reality TV is *so* exciting."

Marci suspected reality TV was an insidious form of hell. "Give me thirty minutes and I'll be ready to go," she said.

"Take as much time as you want. We have all evening."

OVERNIGHT THE TENT genie had erected two huge white structures in the parking lot adjacent to the Museum of Texas Music. Inside one of the tents a crew was setting up long picnic tables for visitors to use after they'd purchased a Texas brisket meal. Another group was assembling barbecue pits big enough to provide food for thousands.

Outside, vendors were engaged in setting up booths

where visitors could entertain their palates with everything from tacos to kettle corn.

The second tent was restricted to contest officials and the twenty finalist teams. After the winners were announced, the public would be allowed in to sample the contestants' cooking.

Marci was shocked by the time and effort the J. W. Watson folks had put into organizing the event. The cooking areas were lined up ten to a side, allowing each team a private booth for preparation. Large refrigerated units run by generators hummed away, allaying her fear of e-coli. One dread down, even though she still had a bunch of concerns—such as how to keep from looking like a total idiot on national TV.

Especially when Larry and Moe, aka Sissy and Harvey, were dueling it out. What in the world was wrong with them? Their bickering drove Marci bonkers, especially since they loved each other.

"What's the problem?" she asked. No answer. They were obviously focused—she'd like to focus on kicking their rear ends all the way to the river.

"Sissy!" she bellowed and was rewarded by a brief cessation of the ongoing argument. "What...is...the... problem?"

"He wants—"

"She's too obstinate—"

Marci held up her hand like a crossing guard. "Are we having a problem trying to figure out where the barbecue pit goes?" she asked sweetly.

In unison Sissy and Harvey nodded.

"Right there." Marci pointed at a spot directly outside the tent flap. "That way we can stay in the shade while we're cooking and still be able to keep the smoke out."

How about that—the dimwits stopped arguing. Considering it was a once-in-a-lifetime event, Marci decided to sneak down to the river to cool off and savor her success. There wasn't anything more peaceful than relaxing by the water.

She wandered down the hill and found a deserted spot under a massive live oak that had spread its leafy branches over the fast-running Guadalupe. Typical of a June day, it was hot, but the light breeze made it pleasant.

Marci felt a comfortable kind of laziness seep right down into her bones. The sound of rushing water and kids' voices calling to each other as they inner tubed on the river was enough to lull her to sleep.

She'd just closed her eyes when a scream ripped apart the aura of peace and quiet. It was a child! Marci jumped to her feet and tried to discover what was wrong. She scanned the water a couple of times before she saw the youngster. He'd obviously strayed from the group that had just floated by.

The boy's tube had obviously flipped and he was now tangled in a submerged tree, his head popping around like a cork in a whirlpool. Marci glanced up and down the riverbank, desperate for help. Crap, there wasn't a soul in sight, so it looked like she was elected.

Marci's lifeguard experience dated from the time dinosaurs roamed the earth. Damn! Where was some young stud when she needed one? Off being young and studly, of course, that was where.

She pulled off her tennis shoes and plunged into the water. She could do this, she told herself, she exercised regularly. Talk about being delusional. Marci hadn't gone fifteen feet before she realized two very important facts—the water was very swift, consequently, they could inner tube in it, and it'd been ages since she'd even been swimming.

Uh, oh!

Every time the child's head came up, he screamed. A few minutes later, his cries were mirrored by the shrieks of a woman, obviously his mother, who was running up and down the bank. The kid was scared, the mother was hysterical and Marci was wondering what it would feel like to drown. Why on God's green earth had she thought she could rescue someone?

Her lungs felt like they were about to explode, but she tucked in her head and forged on. Three feet, two feet, a foot—and then bingo, she grabbed the child's arm. Although he was struggling, she managed to get him into a lifeguard hold. Now she had to determine the shortest distance from point A to point B, and then decide whether they could make it to dry land.

Praise God, someone was yelling, "Hang on. I'm coming."

Her guardian angel was on duty!

Marci managed to wipe the water out of her eyes long enough to sneak a peek. A man was swimming in their direction. When he took the child out of her arms, she breathed a sigh of relief and dog-paddled back to the shore.

By the time they reached the bank, they'd garnered an audience that included EMT personnel. Marci flopped onto the grass and studied her expensive brand-new shorts—her ruined shorts. The near-death experience had to be the reason her teeth were chattering like castanets. God only knew she was too old to play Wonder Woman.

The real hero sat down next to her, and when she turned to thank him, she discovered it was the tall Texan from Live Oak—Johnny something or other. Daniels? No, that was Jack. Walker! Johnny Walker.

For some reason he'd made a fashion transformation. His hair was short, he'd shaved his mustache and he was wearing a pair of shorts that did really nice things for his powerful legs. Not that she was looking at his legs.

Uh, huh!

Chapter Six

Before Marci could get past her "whoa, mama" reaction and form a coherent sentence, her new friend had replaced his sunglasses and plopped an Astros baseball cap on his head. And, he did all that before he even searched for his wallet or put his feet into a scuffed pair of athletic shoes.

If he hadn't jumped in the water when he had, they'd probably be dragging the river for her soggy corpse. When Marci had that epiphany, her body went into hyper-overdrive and started shaking.

"It's okay, really, it's okay," he reassured her in a deep baritone that she could listen to all day long.

"I'm, uh, I'm…" Marci couldn't finish the sentence because she honestly didn't have a clue what she was about to say.

"Shh," he said and put his arms around her shoulders.

For a brief second Marci wanted to sink into his comforting warmth. Post-traumatic stress syndrome had to be the reason she was sitting on a riverbank with a sexy cowboy's arms around her. The excitement that zinged through her body must be the result of an adrenaline overdose.

Uh, huh.

"I thought I was going to have a heart attack," he admitted, then lapsed into a chuckle that sounded like it came from the depths of his soul. "Hero stuff is *not* for old guys."

He still had his arm around her. And wasn't that yummy?

"I was sure I was about to die," Marci said as she ran a hand through her hair to make sure there wasn't a clump of moss in it. Raccoon eyes and river debris— wouldn't that be cute? And why was she worried about her appearance?

"Do you remember me?" he asked, forking his fingers through his hair. "I'm the guy you met in Live Oak."

"I know." Marci smiled at the sheepish expression on his face. "I might be old but my memory works fine."

"I mean with my hair and everything." He did a sweeping motion that encompassed his entire new look. "I, uh," he started to say something, and then paused as he turned to the scene being played out at the riverbank.

Marci took note of the activity. The EMTs were doing their thing and a crowd had gathered to catch the action. People naturally gravitated to where the action was, and these folks weren't any different. Fortunately, the child was sitting up talking to the emergency personnel.

"Let's get out of here. I don't know about you, but I don't want to get involved in doing some sort of paperwork." He stood and reached down to Marci.

That was one of the best ideas she'd heard lately.

"Sure." She took his hand.

He twined his fingers with hers. "Can I treat you to a cup of coffee?"

"Uh, huh." The hand-holding was nice, a bit strange, but pretty darned skin-tingling.

"There's a bakery down the street that makes sweet rolls the size of dinner plates. How about it?" he asked.

There was nothing like a life-threatening incident to heighten the taste buds because Marci's mouth was watering. "Lead the way."

The bakery/coffee shop's cobblestone patio was shaded by a large live oak. Flowers bloomed in abundance, creating a bower of fragrance. It was a perfect place to start the day.

"This is great," Marci commented as she cut another piece of delectable pastry. "Since we'll be here through the weekend, I think I might become a regular patron."

"Would you like to have dinner with me?" he asked.

The fork carrying the sweet roll paused halfway to her mouth. She hadn't had a date since her ill-fated relationship with Mr. "America's Most Wanted."

Marci's most recent foray into the dating scene had ended abruptly when the police discovered that her boyfriend, Bill, and his accomplices had been offing Houston drug dealers. In his defense, he truly believed he was helping law enforcement. But murder? That was a huge lapse in judgment and now he was living the life of a fugitive, presumably in Mexico.

Since that incident, Marci's confidence in her picking ability had taken a nosedive, not that there were many prospects in Port Serenity. Once burned, twice shy and all that rot. However, Johnny *was* incredibly appealing.

"Okay." The answer came out of her mouth before she could stop herself.

"I CAN'T BELIEVE you have a *date*. With *him*," Sissy squealed before she did a jig around the room. "I wouldn't mind finding his boots under *my* bed."

"Sissy!"

"Well, I wouldn't."

"What about Harvey?"

"What about him?" She pouted. "In case you don't remember, we're divorced."

"Uh, huh."

"Well, we are. And there's nothing going on between us."

"If you say so." Marci's ace in the hole was that agreeing with Sissy when she wanted to get into a spat made her sister crazy.

Sure enough, Sissy stomped into her bedroom leaving Marci alone in the living area pondering the wisdom of her "date." Her musing was cut short by the clank and bang of a badly tuned engine. In this upscale enclave of yuppies and CEOs, she suspected that only Johnny Walker would be driving a clunker.

Marci peeked out the curtain and there he was—baseball cap yanked down so far you could barely see his face and the ubiquitous sunglasses obscuring his eyes. Was he trying to go incognito?

When Johnny came in, he did remove the glasses and hat. His gentleman genes were obviously in good working order. That was when she noticed his eyes were a beautiful caramel color flecked with gold. He was more handsome than she remembered, not that she'd had much of a chance to study him. The one time she'd seen him without the shades had been during the near-drowning experience, when she'd been hyperventilating out of sheer terror.

"Where are you guys going?" Sissy asked as she strolled in. Her busybody nature had trumped her snit.

"I thought we could walk over to the Grist Mill."

Johnny answered Sissy's question, but turned to Marci for her opinion. "That is, unless you want German food. They have some great places in New Braunfels. Or you name it and I'm game."

"The Grist Mill sounds good." Marci answered quickly, trying to forestall any embarrassing comment that might be fomenting in Sissy's brain. Swear to goodness, you could dress that girl up; taking her out was the iffy part.

FORTUNATELY A COMBINATION of late-summer sun and dinner al fresco gave Johnny an excuse to keep on the ball cap and sunglasses. His mama was a stickler for good manners, and if she saw him now she'd snatch him bald-headed.

Nope, Mama wouldn't approve, but he had to find out whether his disguise was going to work. Frankly, he'd give it about fifty-fifty odds.

Johnny considered ordering the ribs and then ditched that idea and went with the chicken-fried steak. Everyone knew ribs weren't first-date food. But what did he know about first dates? He hadn't been on one in ages.

"Are you photosensitive?" Marci's question broke into his ruminations concerning dating etiquette.

"What?"

"You keep your sunglasses on all the time. I was just wondering whether you have a problem with your eyes."

Johnny reluctantly removed his shades.

"That's nice. You have very beautiful eyes."

He wasn't sure he wanted to have any part of his anatomy described as beautiful; however, a compliment was a compliment and at the advanced age of fifty-eight, he'd take any kind word he could get.

People assumed fame was always accompanied by an inflated ego. In Johnny's case that couldn't be further from the truth. Even though he appeared in front of thousands of people, he was a private person. In his experience, celebrity was fleeting.

"Thank you," he said, tempted to put the sunglasses in his pocket. However, when he glanced at an adjacent table and saw a woman staring at him, he immediately replaced them. It was too early to reveal his true identity. And for whatever reason, he really wanted to see where this relationship, or whatever it might be, was heading.

"Would you like to go over to the dance hall and do some two-steppin'?" The featured band hadn't started playing, so it was a safe bet he wouldn't bump into any old friends.

"I don't know." Marci shrugged. "I've never done any western dancing."

Johnny picked up her hand and kissed her fingers. "I'll teach you." He smiled at the way she nibbled on her bottom lip.

"I hate looking like a dummy," she admitted.

"I promise we won't look any dumber than anyone else out there stomping around. And no one notices anything but their own feet."

His comment prompted a chuckle from Marci.

"Okay, I'll go, but fair warning. I'm *really* not a dancer."

DURING ITS LIFETIME the Gruene Dance Hall had seen everything from oom pah bands to top country stars. It was now a festival of Stetson hats, tight jeans, big belt buckles and the Texas Two-Step.

Primitive would be a charitable description of this

mecca of country/western music; falling down would be more accurate. Rough plank shutters that were raised in the summer and lowered in the winter constituted the sides of the building, and its last paint job was more than likely done during the Great Depression.

Unfortunately the heating and cooling system was as primitive as the exterior. Screens were all that kept the critters at bay. Long communal picnic tables provided seating, although most folks weren't worried about sitting down.

"Would you like a beer?" Johnny asked as they walked through the bar.

"Yes, thanks." Maybe a beer would help calm her skittery nerves. Dancing, dinner, dating—what *was* she doing?

Johnny discovered a couple of seats in a private corner and then went back to the bar for their drinks. As Marci watched him make his way across the crowded dance floor, she had the brief impression that there was something familiar about him. And that didn't count their Live Oak encounter.

Several people did a double-take and then spoke to him as he was trying to get through the crowd. Each time he shook his head, smiled and didn't break stride.

What was with that?

It was almost fifteen minutes before Johnny returned with two cold beer bottles in his hands. "Here you go." He put hers on the table. "I tried to find some pretzels but didn't have any luck."

"Don't worry about it, I'm stuffed," Marci said as she clinked her longneck with his. "Here's to…here's to whatever." If Letterman had a list of all-time worst toasts, that one would be at the top.

"Yeah, here's to something." He graced her with one of his endearing smiles.

"You ready for your dance lesson?" he asked, bringing her to her feet.

"We'll start with an easy one." He pulled her into his arms. "Hook your fingers in the back of my belt, hang on and follow me."

He was close enough that she could see the golden flecks in his eyes, and when he winked she couldn't help but notice his "to die for" lashes.

"And don't worry about stompin' on my shoes. I'm tough."

Western dancing was much easier than Marci had imagined. Just as he'd said, it was a matter of listening to the beat, hanging on and letting him lead. Much to her surprise, she was having a ball. And being held by a sexy guy wasn't bad, either. After they made about four circles of the dance floor, Marci saw a group forming up to line dance.

"Do you know how to do that?" she asked.

Johnny glanced over his shoulder. "Sure. You want me to teach you?"

Marci paused and then laughed. "Okay, if we can practice over in the corner." Learning a new skill was one thing; looking like a complete idiot was another entirely.

"Done." He danced her past the stage into a dimly lit area. "How about here?"

"It's great." Actually, it was the perfect place for a kiss. The minute that idea entered her brain, she had the urge to thump her cranium. A kiss!

"This is easy. Grab my belt." He set her hand on the belt loop by his hip. "Watch my feet, listen to the music and I'll talk you through it. It's a piece of cake."

"Uh, huh." Right. She'd conquer this one and then send off for a do-it-yourself manual on brain surgery.

"Johnny, my God, is that you?" The voice was a honeyed drawl and very loud. The owner of the voice was young, redheaded and Barbie-doll voluptuous.

"Sugar, what are you doing here? And what's with the shades?" She didn't provide him a chance to answer before she planted a huge kiss right on those sensual lips Marci had been eyeing. Darn! The kid couldn't be over thirty. That sucked.

Johnny went into hyperdrive with that weird head-shaking tic Marci had noticed a couple of times before.

"Bambi. Let me get you a beer." Johnny grabbed the girl's elbow and before Marci could close her mouth they were halfway across the dance floor.

Well, if that didn't beat all. Rude—that was plain rude. What was she thinking? She wouldn't kiss that man if he was the last toad in the swamp.

Chapter Seven

Bambi Belmont was one of Johnny's backup singers and possibly the last person in the world he'd expected to encounter. Damn! Trying to maintain his anonymity was more difficult than wrestling an octopus.

"I have a favor to ask." They found a table in one of the more obscure areas of the crowded bar.

"Just name it and it's yours, boss man." Bambi popped her gum a couple of times before she got a barmaid's attention.

"Two Shiner Bocks, please, ma'am." She placed the order and turned to Johnny. "Okay, what's up? And what's with the yuppie disguise? Sugar, if you weren't like a brother to me, I'd never have recognized you. You look so different."

"That's good. That's real good. I'm trying to make sure the lady I'm with doesn't discover my identity."

"Lady?" Bambi looked puzzled. "You mean that pretty blonde you were dancing with was your date?"

Her comment came out a bit louder than Johnny would've liked.

"Yep, she's my date."

"Oh dude, you are so screwed!" Bambi squealed.

That was when reality hit him like a runaway train. Damn it, she was right. "Stay here. Don't move a muscle. I'll be back." He sprinted across the dance floor, and guess what, she was long gone. Crap!

Johnny stomped back to the bar disregarding any attempt at secrecy.

"She's gone. She's vamoosed."

Bambi put on her ultimate "you are *such* a dummy" expression. "What did you expect? You hauled butt out of there like the devil himself was on your tail." She polished her nails on her shirt. "And you took me with you. Honey, I wouldn't give a plug nickel for your chances with her."

"Oops." She was right. Damn it, she was *so* right.

"Yeah, oops. Now tell me what this is all about and then maybe Mama Bambi can be of some assistance."

Johnny filled her in on how he'd met Marci and laid out his plan to get better acquainted without the junk surrounding fame.

"So she doesn't have a clue who you are?"

"Nope."

"And she doesn't know anything about our business."

"Nope."

"Wow."

"Yes, Bambi, there are one or two people out there who have never heard of Garth or Kenny." Johnny laughed at his own comment. "And believe it or not, they couldn't care less."

"Don't you worry." She patted Johnny's hand. "I'll help Brian spread the word that you're off limits. And if we see any tourists heading your way we'll push 'em in another direction. Think that'll work?"

Johnny certainly hoped so.

"Now…" She snapped her gum and smirked. "You've got some grovelin' to do. Yes sir, you're gonna be doing some world-class knee crawlin'.

Wasn't that the truth?

"I need some help because it's been a long time for me," he said.

"Oh, my God!" she shrieked as her face turned the color of her hair.

"I don't mean *that*." Johnny snorted. "I mean, what's the protocol for dating these days? Do I send her dozens of roses or what?"

Bambi grinned as she got into the spirit of the situation. "You're supposed to be poor, right?"

"Uh, huh."

"Then you should do something hokey and romantic. A bunch of wildflowers would be perfect. Johnny Walker wouldn't be able to afford roses from a florist."

He hadn't thought of that. "Are wildflowers in season?"

"I doubt it, but don't you worry. I'll come up with a great plan."

That was supposed to make Johnny feel confident? Bambi's wicked sense of humor was legendary. She'd played some truly ingenious tricks on the other band members.

"And if all else fails, we'll steal a single rose out of someone's yard."

Yep, that was *exactly* what he was afraid of.

JOHNNY FELT LIKE the biggest dummy in Texas—and why not? He was standing on the front step of Marci's cottage holding a single rose that, thanks to Bambi's sneaky method of acquisition, would probably earn him a thumping by an irate senior. Good God, he was too old for this.

He rapped on the door. Bambi said groveling was the key. He could do that as long as it didn't involved getting down on one knee. *That* would be tough.

Sissy cracked the door open. "What do you want?"

Nope, didn't sound very friendly. He took off his Astros cap, barely resisting the urge to twist it. "Um, I'd like to apologize to Marci." He held up the rose. "Is she here?"

Without answering, Sissy grabbed the flower and slammed the door in his face.

Failure was somewhat of a foreign concept, but this time he was afraid he'd met it. What would Bambi do? Johnny thought about his redheaded friend with her fiery Irish temper. Giving up was *not* an option. Johnny turned on his heel and went in search of Bambi and some advanced dating tips.

SISSY HANDED Marci a yellow rose that had seen better days. "I'll bet he stole it out of someone's yard," she pronounced.

Marci smiled. "Isn't that sweet? Is he still out there?" she mouthed.

Sissy did a surreptitious check. "Nope, he's gone," she said and then fell onto the couch and started laughing. "It's pitiful." She paused. "And very romantic. So what are you planning to do the next time you see him?"

"I don't know that there'll be a next time."

"Of course there'll be a next time. He told you he's working as a roadie for the Vince McDowell band, didn't he?"

"Yes."

"Did you know that Vince McDowell's band is playing at every one of the cook-offs?"

"Are you kidding?" Marci asked. She was astonished at all the things she didn't know about this upcoming debacle. So Mr. Johnny Walker would be around for at least a month.

Was that good, or was that bad?

Considering the way her heart went into arrhythmia whenever she saw him, he might prove to be the death of her.

Chapter Eight

The cook-off was a study in country kitsch, and as much as Marci hated to admit it, the experience was turning out to be a lot of fun. It had all the elements of a great party—enthusiastic folks, good country music, kicker dancing and delicious food.

The competitors started cooking the briskets and ribs well before dawn because authentic Texas barbecue required hours of smoking the meat over a mesquite fire. Consequently, mouthwatering smells filled the air inside the huge white tent as Marci and Sissy put the final touches on their barbecue basting sauce.

"Honeybun, we're going to mingle with some of the other finalists," Sissy informed Harvey before she gave him a swat on the rear. "Be sure to use lots of sauce."

"Yes, ma'am." Harvey gave his ex an affectionate mock salute.

Pray to God Sissy could maintain some kind of decorum for four weeks—four very long weeks—because everything that was said and done inside that tent would be fodder for the TV cameras. Even though there were only four technicians, it felt as if Big Brother was watching. And Marci *really* didn't want to look like a country hick on TV.

"Let's go say hi to our new neighbors." Sissy pulled her along to meet and greet some of the other teams.

"I'm Sissy Aguirre and this is my sister, Marci Hamilton."

Their neighbor was vintage Chef Boyardee, complete with a big belly, tall white hat and jovial smile.

"Pleased to meet you ladies." He stuck out a hand covered in a latex glove. "I'm Timmy, Timmy O'Connor, and this is my partner, Barton." Barton was as thin as Timmy was round, although they were both wearing similar white hats. "We're from Dallas," Timmy continued as he waved a wooden spoon in the air.

He was obviously the spokesman of the duo.

"I come from a long line of New Orleans chefs. This was a natural for us. We want to use the money to open our own restaurant."

And Marci wanted to use the money to buy a fancy car. Talk about feeling trite.

After what seemed like an interminable session of Timmy's chatter, Marci and Sissy gently extricated themselves. The man was rumor central; he seemed to know everything about everybody. Although Marci suspected that what he didn't know, he made up.

The folks on the other side of their booth were a married couple from Throckmorton, a tiny town in the Texas Panhandle. Bud was a retired butcher and Mabel owned a beauty shop. From the smell of things, they had Texas barbecue down pat.

Sissy was about to move on to Idabelle Cornell's booth when Marci grabbed her arm. "I don't trust that woman. There's something about her that gives me the heebie-jeebies. So for right now, let's concentrate on getting our sauce act together. Harvey could probably use some help."

"Oh, okay," Sissy acquiesced and followed her sister back to their stove. They'd spent the morning making sure the sauce was perfect.

"So what else do we need to do?" Sissy asked as she lifted the lid on the Dutch oven and leaned over for a big sniff.

"Nothing," Marci mumbled. "I just needed to get away from him." She pointed at the ever-present cameraman, who'd wandered off to film the crowd. Every time he swung the camera in their direction, Marci had to resist the urge to scamper off. The guys next door didn't seem to have the same problem. In fact, with his jiggling belly and rumbling laugh, Timmy (aka Chef Boyardee) was thriving on the publicity.

Sissy stuck her head outside the tent. "Harvey, is that meat about ready? And are you sure you've basted it enough?" she asked.

Jeez. The man was a saint.

"Positively," he answered as he dropped a brisket on the butcher block. Harvey was wearing a huge apron that had the J. W. Watson Sure Fire Sauce logo emblazoned on the front. Sissy and Marci were wearing miniversions of the same apron.

"Let's slice it," he said, brandishing a knife that could easily hack through a jungle. "We have people waiting to get in for a taste." Each team was asked to provide enough small individual samples of their culinary talent to satisfy the hordes of curious spectators.

People of every size and shape were waiting to get into the tent, but before the masses were allowed entry, the judges would come by to do their tasting. They were the culinary experts who held Marci's dream, albeit rather banal, of a VW convertible in their hands.

"Timmy." Marci had to raise her voice in order for her neighbor to hear. "Who's the guy with the ponytail? The one all the cameras are following,"

"*Ma chere*, are you kidding with old Timmy?" Apparently Marci's IQ had fallen in his estimation. "Um, no."

"That, my sweetness, is Vince McDowell." Timmy fanned himself. "He's the guru of all things country."

So *that* was the famous Vince McDowell. Holy cow, he was scraggly. And not only that, he was short. Didn't seem to bother his ego, though.

The leer he leveled at Sissy was downright lascivious.

"And who do we have here?" Vince asked one of his entourage.

"These lovely ladies are Sissy Aguirre and Marci Hamilton. They're our entrants from Port Serenity."

The man doing the introductions was Brian, J. W. Watson's business manager, and the organizer of this little event.

"Sweet." The singer almost purred his response. "I'm Vince McDowell, and it's my pleasure, totally my delight," he cooed, taking Sissy's hand and caressing it as if they were lovers.

Oh, boy! Harvey was about to go postal and who could blame him. Marci was tempted to smack the singer—until, that is, she came to her senses. Assaulting the friend of the guy offering the prize money would seriously diminish her chances for a brand-new VW convertible. Darn.

So instead, she snatched Sissy's hand away from the

old lech. "It's been really nice meeting you, Mr. McDowell, but my sister and I are busy getting ready for the judges."

Sissy stared at her hand with the look of a woman emerging from a trance. "Um, huh, we have to cook."

"Miss Sissy, I'll be seein' ya soon, very soon." Vince winked before he sauntered off.

Marci popped her sister on the arm. "Get a grip," she muttered, as Harvey stomped off to check on the meat. Poor guy probably needed a little alone time.

"What do you *mean*?" Sissy was using her snotty voice.

"I mean cut the crap and concentrate on the contest."

"I think he's cute."

"You have *got* to be kidding!" Marci exclaimed. "He's nose-high to your cleavage."

Sissy put on the smirk Marci had learned to hate in childhood.

"That might be interesting," she said.

"Spare me, please." Marci dredged up the last of her patience. "The judges will be here in fifteen minutes. We have to get crackin'. And you'd better play nice with Harvey. He's pissed off."

"Yeah, yeah, right." Sissy sashayed over to her ex and gave him a smacking kiss.

Relatives could be such a pain, and Marci's were particularly tiresome.

Back to the business of winning the stupid contest— the sauce was simmering, the meat was ready and their display was lovely. Marci glanced at the other booths and was pleased to note that with the fresh flowers and colorful tablecloths, their display was a veritable fiesta marooned in a sea of longnecks.

Marci had stepped outside the tent for a breath of

fresh air when the cell phone in her pocket rang. It was Amanda, who responded with a squeal.

"Hi, Mee Maw. Guess what?" she giggled.

Marci couldn't resist a smile. That granddaughter of hers was such a cutie. "What?"

"I have my own cell phone! Isn't that the coolest thing you've ever heard?"

"Very cool." And quite unexpected, since Lolly had refused to even discuss the subject.

"And you're the first person I called."

"Is that okay with your mom?"

"Sure. She said I can only use it for talking to you, calling home and emergencies. Mama said I have some kind of restricted plan."

Marci could envision Amanda waving her hand in a "whatever" fashion.

"How did you talk your mom into getting you a phone?"

The pause on the other end of the line told most of the story—and more than likely it wasn't going to be a pretty one.

"Well…the other day Bren was supposed to pick me up from piano lessons, but I waited and waited and he didn't come."

Now they were getting to the nitty gritty.

"So I decided to walk home and I was about halfway there when Sergeant Joe drove by and picked me up."

"Amanda Lavinia! Tell me, *please* tell me, you didn't plan to walk five miles down a busy highway." When kids hit puberty did *all* their common sense vanish?

"Um, yeah."

"Then what happened?"

Another pause. "Bren got in bad trouble. He was at the Tastee Freeze with Missy Carter and forgot about me."

Oh, dear.

"Did you get in trouble?"

"Yeah, um, well I'm sorta grounded. But what was I supposed to do? Sit around and wait?" She spoiled her angst by giggling. "I did get a phone, though."

"Yes, you did." It was hard to stay annoyed with her. And "sorta grounded" probably meant the child would be sequestered until her thirtieth birthday.

"I gotta go. I'm running up my minutes. I had to tell you about my phone. Even Leslie doesn't have one." Amanda finished her monologue concerning telecommunications and then added, "Are you having a good time?"

"Yes, I am, but I miss you."

"I miss you, too. Love you, bye."

"Bye, sweetie. Kiss your sisters and give Bren a hug."

"Okay."

Marci snapped the phone shut. Although she *was* having a good time she did miss her family. The cell chirped again.

"Did you forget something?" she asked.

Silence.

"Hello." Marci waited for someone to answer. All she heard was static.

"Hello." There was more crackling and then some garbled Spanish.

"Hello?"

Nothing. Marci closed the phone. This wasn't the first strange call she'd had and it was beginning to make her nervous.

"Did Sissy give you the flower?"

Marci turned around and there he was, leaning

against a tree. One look at the long, tall Texan and concerns about weird calls faded to the background.

"Um, yes, she did."

"And?" He straightened up and walked toward her, palm out. "Are you planning to stay mad at me, or will I have to raid someone else's garden?"

She always did admire a man with a sense of humor. "So you really did steal that flower?"

"Sort of."

"Sort of?"

He paused before he answered. "Sort of means I was chicken, so someone else did the actual deed. I was an accomplice after the fact."

How could you not like him? She put her hand in his upturned palm and he immediately closed his fingers around hers.

He gently tugged her toward the shady path that led to river and away from the growing crowd.

"How's the cook-off going?"

"Okay, I guess. The judges are coming in a little bit, and Sissy and Harvey are bickering. All's well with the world."

"Can you sit with me for a few minutes? I'd like to explain something." He sat down in the grass and pulled her alongside him.

"Sure." Why not? Her curiosity was getting the best of her.

"I was rude last night."

"Oh, yeah."

"And I'm terribly sorry. Would you like some chocolate or more flowers, maybe?"

"Chocolate would be good. However, what I'd really like is an explanation. Even when I was young and dating, I never had someone run out like their shirt was on fire."

Johnny winced. "Well, that was a huge mistake." He rubbed his temple as if he had a bad headache. "Bambi's an old friend and I had something important to tell her."

"Honestly?"

"Honestly, she's like a daughter to me." He gave a self-deprecating laugh. "You don't think I'd be interested in someone that young, do you?"

"Lots of men would be."

"I'm not lots of men."

Wasn't that the truth! She'd known him for less than a week and already she knew there was a special quality about him.

"Why was she so surprised to see you?"

That was a tough question, especially since Marci was too smart to fall for a bunch of baloney.

"She didn't expect me to be here because I spend a lot of time in Nashville."

"Really? I thought you worked on a ranch."

"I do." He wondered how much he could tell her without lying. "Sometimes I do," he added.

"That doesn't make much sense."

He could tell she wasn't impressed with his explanation. Not that he blamed her. It sounded pretty lame to him, too.

Johnny turned her hand over and kissed the base of each finger. He was almost as shocked at his spontaneous action as she seemed to be. "Can we start over? Let me make it up to you? I promise you won't be sorry."

Although he was encouraged by her smile, he'd bet dollars to doughnuts she'd make him pay. And was he ever right about that.

"I think you owe me a night on the town."

"Okay…"

"In San Antonio. I want to go to dinner on the River Walk."

That he could do. In fact, he knew the perfect place— a restaurant with white tablecloths, candles, privacy and best of all, very few tourists.

Chapter Nine

"Where have you been?" Sissy snapped. On a good hair day, her locks were spiky. Now they looked as if she'd been running her fingers through them over and over again.

"I went for a walk." Little Miss Nosy Nellie didn't need to know about her date with Johnny. Not yet, anyway.

"The judges will be here in a few minutes."

"I know." Marci patted her sister's hand. "Take a deep breath. Don't worry, we'll do fine."

Harvey draped an arm around his ex-wife. "Sweetie, don't get your knickers in a twist. The judges are gonna love you."

THE GOOD NEWS WAS that the sisters won third place and accrued points toward the total prize. The bad news was that they'd only come in third. At least that was Sissy's current rant. Then she changed her tune and broached the subject of Johnny Walker. Sissy tended to get grumpy when she didn't win, so Marci decided to put the woman on ignore. Johnny Walker was *not* going to be a topic of conversation. Yeah, right.

"I can't believe you have a date with *him*."

Marci couldn't believe it, either. She also couldn't

believe how excited she was. He'd told her to dress up. Unfortunately, she had no idea whether he meant dress up for Denny's or for a five-star restaurant. As a compromise, she paired a pencil-thin black skirt with a black sleeveless turtleneck.

"So where are you going?"

"I don't know. Somewhere on the River Walk."

"Take some money. I think most of those places are expensive."

Marci was contemplating ways to thump her sister when there was a tap on the door. Saved by the bell, or in this case, knock.

"I'll get it." Marci jumped up to preempt Sissy's getting there first. She opened the door and almost dropped her teeth.

"Wow!"

It was Johnny. It had to be. What happened to the man in the ball cap and sunglasses? This guy had the same gorgeous brown eyes and short-cropped hair, but he was wearing an elegant charcoal-gray suit and highly polished boots.

"You look fantastic," Marci commented when she could finally get her mouth to work properly.

"Thanks. So do you." A flush worked up his neck to his cheeks.

How about that? Her compliment had embarrassed him.

"I borrowed a car so you wouldn't have to climb into the pickup."

Marci appreciated that. Even though her skirt had a slit, she was afraid that hoisting herself up into his truck would have bared her backside to one and all.

Wouldn't *that* have been cute?

ON THE RIDE INTO San Antonio, Marci and Johnny discussed myriad subjects and found that they agreed on almost everything. This was considerably better than her track record with Sissy. Much as she loved her sister, they disagreed on virtually every topic.

She was about to ask what he thought of the Dallas Cowboys when her cell phone rang. Caller ID showed the now-familiar *out of area* indication. Although she'd only had two calls, it was two too many. They were all similar—a lot of static, some kind of garbled talking, some Spanish music in the background, and then the line would disconnect. Her first thought had been it was Bill, but she immediately dismissed that idea.

"Hello." No answer. "Hello." She said it with more emphasis and when there was again no answer, she snapped the phone closed.

"A problem?"

"Yes, no. I don't know. I've gotten a couple of calls that show up as *out of the area* and when I answer, no one's there. It's creepy."

"You should contact the phone company. I'm sure they can trace them or block them or something."

Marci smiled. "If it continues, I'll do that. Right now it's not bad enough for me to make it into a federal case. I could always turn off my phone." Marci was determined not to let her phantom caller spoil her evening. "So, where are we going?"

"I've made reservations at the Lemon Tree in La Villita. I hope that's okay."

Whoa! Corrine Baker, a friend from Port Serenity, had been to the Lemon Tree. Although Corrine was prone to exaggeration, she'd been quite specific that it was mongo expensive and *very* elegant. Could a cowboy who drove a beater pickup really afford a place like that? And how could Marci suggest a cheaper restaurant without hurting his feelings?

"I'm not really dressed for anything that fancy." That was the truth and nothing but the truth.

"You'll be the most beautiful woman there."

Gee, he sounded like he really meant it. That type of compliment was enough to turn a girl's head.

NESTLED ON THE BANKS of the San Antonio River, La Villita was the city's original neighborhood, originally built as a cluster of tents for the Spanish soldiers stationed at Mission San Antonio Valero, later called the Alamo. The "little village" was the epicenter of revolutionary activities during the Texas revolution and then the site of Santa Anna's cannon line at the Battle of the Alamo.

From that humble beginning, La Villita had evolved into a National Historic District and a "must see" on any trip to the San Antonio River Walk. Strolling the old brick-and-tile-paved streets of the shady oasis was like a trip back two centuries. Tourists and locals browsed through shops, watched craftsmen at work, feasted on foods from around the world and enjoyed the stately trees and colorful beds of seasonal flowers.

"Here we are." Johnny parked in a self-service lot adjacent to the village. "I'd really rather not do valet, if you don't mind."

"No, I don't mind at all." And she'd be even more comfortable if they were going someplace in a lower price range. "Sure you don't want to go to Dirty Nellie's?" she asked, referring to the Irish pub famous for its selection of international beer.

Johnny smiled as if he knew what she was up to. "No,

I'd rather go to the Lemon Tree." He got out of the car and came around to the passenger side.

It had been eons since she'd been the recipient of such gallantry, so she felt compelled to comment. "Your mama taught you manners."

"Yes, ma'am. She sure did."

On the way to the restaurant they strolled by stores featuring hand-woven fashions, antiques, hand-blown glass and jewelry.

"I love this part of Texas, don't you?" she asked.

Johnny had to laugh. The last time he was at La Villita, he was doing a concert at the Arneson River Theater, and he'd barely escaped the hordes of fans. A leisurely stroll with Marci was much more entertaining.

"Have you ever been here for A Night in Old San Antonio?" He referred to a week during Fiesta when tens of thousands of people converged on the village.

"No. I heard you need to be pretty tough to make it through that one."

"Yeah, I haven't done it since college, and that was a million years ago."

His comment brought Marci back to the question she'd been meaning to ask, although she wasn't convinced she was ready for the answer.

"When did you go to college?" That seemed like a subtle way to find out how old he was.

"I graduated in 1970."

Okay, that put him around fifty-seven or fifty-eight. Damn! Almost five years younger than she was. Crumb!

Marci was so busy thinking about their discrepancy in age that she stumbled on one of the cobblestones.

He steadied her by grabbing her elbow. Then he slid

his arm around her. "You'd better be careful. You don't want to fall."

He probably meant she didn't want to take a tumble and break a hip—seeing that she was so old and everything.

"Hmmph."

"Uh, oh. What did I do?" he asked as he drew her closer.

"What do you mean?" Was that snotty voice really hers?

"I mean in my experience when a woman says 'hmmph' like you just did, some guy's in big trouble." He lifted her hair and kissed the side of her neck. "So why don't you put old Johnny out of his misery and tell him what he did."

The kiss was nice; in fact, it was quite delectable. Marci savored it a few minutes before she came to her senses. She felt like Mrs. Robinson—well, not exactly, but five years was five years. Plus, she had to remember that her previous male friend had his picture on a post office wall.

"I'm older than you are."

"So what?"

"So, I'm old enough to be your older sister."

Johnny stopped under an ancient oak and enticed her into his arms. "Believe me, I don't think of you as a sister. I wouldn't want to kiss any of my relatives like I want to kiss you."

His hand caressed the back of her neck as his head came slowly, very slowly down. Against her better judgment, Marci wrapped her arms around him. At first his lips were soft. But it took only a few seconds for the kiss to become demanding and devouring.

The screech of teenage laughter abruptly brought them back to reality.

"Oh." Marci could barely breathe, much less put together a coherent thought.

"Yeah, oh." He rested his forehead against hers. "I guess we shouldn't be doing this in public."

No, they definitely shouldn't be. But it was nice to feel young and attractive. Marci smiled and put her arm through his. "Let's have dinner."

"Yes, ma'am. I think you'll like this place."

The spicy aroma wafting from the white adobe building was scrumptious.

"Smells wonderful."

"Oh, yes," Johnny said. The next part would be tricky. He was a frequent patron of the Lemon Tree, and he knew they were incredibly circumspect. In fact, he'd talked to the manager when he made the reservation and had his assurance they'd have a private room. Still, there was always a possibility that someone would slip up.

When they strolled in, the maitre d' rushed to greet them. "Mr.—"

Johnny cut him off before he could come out with the name Watson. "Walker. Johnny Walker."

The maitre d' took a step back as he regained his composure. "Certainly. Follow me, please, Mr. Walker, Madame." He nodded at Marci. "We have your table ready." He seated them in an alcove and handed them embossed menus and a wine list before he bowed and scraped his way out of the little room.

"What's with him?" Marci asked. "He acted like we're important. That's silly."

"They treat everyone like that. It's the policy of the management."

"How do you know?"

"My cousin worked as a waiter here when he was going to Trinity University. You should hear some of his stories."

Marci picked up the menu and almost had a coronary when she saw the prices. Talk about wanting an arm and a leg—these folks were after the whole torso. "Are you *positive* you want to eat here?" She had to give him one last chance to make a getaway. If he didn't take it, they could at least go Dutch treat. Although she suspected talking him into *that* would be harder than making water into wine.

"Absolutely. So relax and enjoy yourself. We can always wash dishes if we have to." He paused before he gave her one of his lopsided grins.

"I'm just teasing," he told her when her mouth dropped open.

Chapter Ten

"Tell me all about your date. And I do mean *all*," Sissy demanded as she threw her overnighter in the back of the convertible and jumped into the driver's seat.

Sissy had been in bed when Marci got home, and this morning they'd been busy getting packed to go to Luckenbach.

When they were teenagers, the sisters had shared everything; however, this time Marci wasn't sure she wanted to discuss Johnny. Their fledgling relationship was special, and somehow fragile.

"We went to dinner at the Lemon Tree."

"The Lemon Tree," Sissy squeaked. "Is it as nice as I've heard? And how can a guy who works as a roadie afford an expensive restaurant like that?"

"Yes, it's lovely and the food was fantastic. As far as the second question goes, I don't know. I kept hinting that we should go someplace cheaper and he wouldn't listen. And when I tried to pay for my half, he about had a fit."

"Hmm."

"My sentiments exactly," Marci said as she settled back in the soft leather seat to enjoy the scenery.

They were taking a short cut across the Texas Hill

Country to Fredericksburg—Luckenbach's next-door
neighbor and one of Marci's favorite places.

The Hill Country was rural charm epitomized with
its outcroppings of limestone rocks, vistas of scrub oak
and mesquite, lazy meandering rivers and a culture
firmly rooted in its German heritage. Natives and
visitors alike were entranced by the wild beauty.

In 1836 following the creation of the Republic of
Texas, the founding fathers looked to Europe for new
settlers. The theory was that if they offered free land,
immigrants would come. And by gosh, they came—
Germans, French, Poles, Czechs, Swiss, Danes, Swedes
and Norwegians.

The first colonists to settle Fredericksburg were each
given ten acres of farmland and a town lot. Religion
played an important part in the lives of these early
settlers, so they used their properties in town to build
Sunday houses. Many of those homes still stood, providing Fredericksburg with its quaint ambiance.

"I love this place," Marci commented as Sissy turned
onto the main street. With its century-old buildings,
mélange of B&Bs and wineries, boutiques featuring
both handcrafts and designer items and, yep, redneck
bars, the small city was a gathering place for well-heeled
visitors and local ranchers alike. Shiny German imports
vied with pickups sporting rifle racks for the few
parking spots on the crowded street.

"Look at all the people," Sissy said, indicating the
sidewalks packed with tourists intent on immersing
themselves in a little bit of Europe, Texas style.

"It'll be worse this weekend."

"You're right," Sissy said, turning down a side street.
"Can you tell from the map where our inn is located?"

Marci snorted. Her read a map? "Our directions say the Peach Tree Inn is across the street from the Pacific War Museum. Did you see anything resembling a museum?"

"Nope. But everything's on this main drag. I'll go around the block and drive slow so you can look."

"Okay."

"There it is," Marci said suddenly. "It's gorgeous." Nestled under the shade of a huge oak tree, it was picturesque with limestone walls and tin roof.

Sissy nodded in agreement. "I wonder when Harvey will get here."

Harvey had told them he'd stop by Luckenbach and leave the barbecue pit. Considering the limited parking around the inn, that had been one of their smarter moves.

"After we get settled, I want to go to Luckenbach to check out the facilities," Sissy said.

"Sounds like a plan."

RUNNING OUT to Luckenbach turned out to be more difficult than either of them imagined.

Directionally impaired though Marci was, she found Luckenbach on the map with no problem. Now if she could find it on the road, they'd have it made. For years the famous dance hall had been a center for Texan country/western fans, so why weren't there any signs?

"I guess if you don't know where you're going you don't need to get there, huh?" Marci had reverted to sarcasm. "I know this is the road, but I expected to see some kind of sign before now."

"Me, too," Sissy muttered. "I'm really surprised there wasn't something where we turned off the main highway."

"Yeah. Oh, look—there it is." Marci indicated a sign reading Luckenbach/Cannon City. "Go right."

Sissy slowed and turned onto a poorly paved road. "Are you positive about this?"

Marci shrugged. "It's the only indication I've seen that Luckenbach is located anywhere in this county."

"Okay, we'll give it a shot."

As they drove, the road got progressively narrower until all of a sudden it became a gravel drive.

Sissy stopped the car and glared at her sister. "Somehow I don't think this is the right way."

"So sue me." Marci tossed her the map. "Find it yourself." Unfortunately they'd made several turns, each getting them deeper into the hinterland.

Sissy grabbed the map and smacked Marci over the head with it. "Does this feel like déjà vu? I'm beginning to think we're a prototype for dumb blond jokes."

Marci laughed and Sissy was forced to join her. "At least we're not almost out of gas."

"Thank goodness for small favors," Sissy said.

"And that *is* how we met Johnny."

"Yep. One of these days you're going to thank your lucky stars we got lost," Sissy proclaimed.

"We'll see."

"Now that sounds like our mother."

Marci laughed at that observation. It was Mother's way of giving a negative reply without actually saying no.

"So, either hand me the map or figure out where we are," Marci said.

"I have a better idea."

"What?"

"We'll ask her." Sissy pointed at a jogger decked out in hot pink spandex. "Have you ever seen anyone that old move that fast?"

"No, can't say I have." The woman had to be at least

ninety and she was picking 'em up and putting 'em down. "I hope she's not lost."

"Me, too." Sissy waved to get her attention. "Ma'am, ma'am." She waited until the jogger drew even with the convertible before she asked the big question. "We're lost. Can you tell us how to get to Luckenbach?"

"Sure can," the woman answered as she leaned into Sissy's window. "You have to follow my directions very specifically or you'll get lost. That stupid sheriff of ours might look and look and never find you." She ended her ominous prediction with a cackle.

Shades of Dorothy and Toto—they'd somehow managed to stumble onto the Wicked Witch of the West.

Chapter Eleven

"Slow down! I think we passed the dance hall."

"Where?" Sissy yelled to be heard over the sound of the engine. "I didn't see anything."

Although Sissy seemed doubtful, she dropped her speed from seventy to sixty.

Lord, that woman had a lead foot.

"Back there." Marci pointed over her shoulder. "The crazy woman said you had to turn right before you got to Grape Creek and we just crossed a bridge."

Sissy stopped on the shoulder of the road and stared at Marci. "Did you see anything, and I mean *anything*, that looked like it would be a draw for tourists?"

"Nope," Marci admitted. "I didn't. But we crossed a bridge. I'm beginning to think this place is nothing more than a figment of someone's imagination."

"I'm with you on that one." Sissy reluctantly turned the car around to retrace their route.

"Go slow," Marci instructed as she kept an eye out for the elusive dance hall. "There it is," she exclaimed, gesturing at the weather-beaten sign that read Luckenbach, Where Everybody's Somebody.

Sissy headed down the gravel road and skidded to a

stop. "You have got to be kidding me! Where's the parking lot? Where are the bathrooms? Where's the anything?"

"Beats me." The entire complex consisted of a large park bordering a dry creek bed, a ramshackle barn and a falling down shack with a U.S. Post Office sign nailed to the porch. It was like expecting to see George Clooney and getting Pee Wee Herman instead.

Marci's research had indicated the Luckenbach post office/general store/beer joint was built in 1866 by an itinerant German preacher. At first glance it seemed the only improvement they'd made since that time was the addition of a couple of porta-potties.

"Maybe it looks better close up." In a pig's eye!

Sissy parked in front of the so-called Post Office. "Surely the big-name dudes who make millions don't come down here to play gigs at that—" she waved a hand in the air "—that dump."

"It is kind of primitive."

"I've seen outhouses that look better." Sissy frowned. "I guess it really doesn't matter because the cook-off will be held over there." She waved a hand in the direction of the park, where several large flatbed trucks were located. "I don't know how we missed those folks." She was referring to a television van and the eighteen-wheeler carrying Vince McDowell's equipment.

"Yeah." Marci was saved from any further observations when Harvey came out of the post office.

"Harv!" Sissy jumped out of the car and engaged her ex in a lip lock.

For goodness sake! Marci grabbed her purse and stomped into the store. Supposedly there was a bar at the back of the place. A Shiner Bock sounded mighty good. Dealing with Sissy for several hours was enough to make a girl thirsty.

"Oh, dear." She stopped at the threshold of the "bar" and gaped. She'd stumbled on the mother lode of southern tacky. Signs, hats and Texas trinkets covered every flat surface in the small room.

"Marci, over here." It wasn't difficult to find the owner of the voice that had been haunting her dreams. And this time he was wearing his sunglasses and a burnt orange University of Texas baseball hat.

"I see you're in your double-oh-eight disguise." She tweaked the bill of his cap as she claimed the adjacent stool.

JOHNNY GRINNED. He'd put out the word about his transformation from J. W. Watson to Johnny Walker. Now all he had to do was avoid stray dimwits who could blow his cover.

"You're here early."

"Yes, we checked into our room and came out to see the facilities." She smiled, remembering their recent jaunt through the hinterland. "Actually we got lost. More than likely we'd still be out there if we hadn't met a nutty old woman who gave us directions. She about scared the heck out of me."

"Was she about four feet tall and as old as Methuselah?"

"Yes. Do you know her?"

Johnny laughed as he folded his hand around hers. "That's Crazy Sally. She's been around these parts since Christ was a corporal. She's harmless, although I've heard she's a crackerjack at potions and voodoo dolls."

Marci faked a shudder. "Our misadventure reminded

me of a horror movie where the clueless female wanders
into a town populated by werewolves."

"Naw. Vampires maybe, but not werewolves.
They're not real."

Johnny was enjoying the banter when out of the corner
of his eye he saw Brian. Their plan was to have a chat with
Vince and then adjourn the business meeting to Johnny's
house in Kerrville. Brian raised his hand in greeting;
however, the minute he recognized Marci he changed direction and found a stool at the other end of the bar.

"How about a beer? I hear their wine comes out of a
paper box."

"A beer's great." Marci placed her purse on the floor.

"Two Shiner Bocks," Johnny told the bartender and
returned his attention to Marci. "I only have time for one
drink and then I have to go to work." He was still
holding her hand. Although his previous dating experience was a distant memory, Johnny felt he was about to
get the hang of it.

Her cheeks took on a nice rosy glow. That was cool.
She wasn't immune to him.

"Tell me again what you do for Vince."

How did he answer that without reverting to a lie? A
minor omission was okay, but he suspected a bold-faced
prevarication wouldn't go over well.

"A little of this and a little of that."

"So you're not really a cowboy."

"I work on the ranch occasionally." If his luck held,
she'd assume he was talking about Vince's ranch. Boy,
was that a laugh. Vince's sole relationship with a cow
was when it was served medium rare and accompanied
by a baked potato.

"What do you do for him when he's on tour?"

"I'm his logistics guy. You sure are a curious miss." He kissed her hand, not only because he wanted to distract her, but because he loved to touch her.

"Okay, I'll drop it for now," she agreed with a sigh. "Don't think you'll get away with being evasive for very long. I taught school so I have great interrogation skills."

He hoped she wasn't as skilled at ferreting out secrets as she thought she was.

"Are you staying in Fredericksburg?"

Johnny stifled a chuckle. She wasn't kidding about conducting an inquisition.

"I have access to a mountain cabin in Kerrville. I'm staying there for the week." He didn't bother to tell her the so-called cabin was named La Montana and had four thousand square feet, a 360-degree view of the Guadalupe Valley and two guest cottages. And it all belonged to him.

"Would you like to go out tonight? I know a great Mexican food restaurant," he said, anxious to be alone with her again. It had been ages since a woman, any woman, had dominated his thoughts and dreams like Marci did.

"I'd love to," she answered. She set her empty beer bottle on the bar and traced some carved letters with one finger.

"Isn't that sweet?" she murmured. "Stan loves Sherry, 1970. What do you suppose happened to Stan and Sherry?"

When Marci smiled at him she captured another piece of his heart.

"I'll bet they got married and have a passel of grand-kids," she went on. "What do you think?" she asked.

"I think if they got married and stayed married, they're really lucky." Call him a cynic, but solid marriages were hard to find, especially in show business.

"That's not very romantic. If…" She blinked a few times, as if she was trying to keep from crying. "Never mind."

Johnny ran his fingers through her silky hair and gently massaged the back of her neck.

"I'm an excellent listener."

"I know you are and I didn't intend to put a damper on things. I was simply going to say that if my husband hadn't been killed, we'd still be married."

Her husband was killed? Johnny had assumed she was divorced.

"Do you want to tell me what happened?"

She hesitated a moment, and then apparently decided to share her story.

"My husband's name was Trey. He was a policeman and he was shot as he tried to give a traffic ticket." Marci sighed. "When the police chief stopped in front of the house, I knew my world was about to fall apart. Lolly, my daughter, was a teenager at the time. I'm not sure I would've made it without her." She paused to take a sip of his beer. "Did I tell you she's the police chief of Port Serenity?"

"No, you didn't tell me that. I'll bet you're proud of her."

"I am. When she first went into law enforcement I was upset, to say the least. Since then, I've managed to adjust, and I'm very pleased with what she's made of her life. Now—" she tickled his jaw "—you have to get to work and I need to find Sissy. Swear to goodness, I can't let her out of my sight for more than two minutes."

Johnny caught her fingers and held them against his face. "What time should I pick you up?"

Marci looked at her watch. "How about six? I have

to get back to the room early tonight. We have a busy day tomorrow."

"Okay." Johnny released her hand as he stood. He could see that Brian was getting antsy. "Dress casually, jeans would be good." He kissed her cheek and wondered if he was in over his head. That pesky *L* word seemed to be flitting through his addled brain at the most inopportune moments—like right this minute.

Chapter Twelve

"So the pretty lady in Luckenbach is the reason you're running all over South Texas when you should be home taking care of business," Brian commented as he retrieved a beer from the wet bar and settled down on one of the comfy chairs ringing Johnny's flagstone patio.

"Uh-huh," Johnny muttered, his attention drawn to the vista before him. From this vantage point it seemed he could see forever. It was a place where time stood still, where cars and traffic were nonexistent, where the song of the mourning dove greeted the morning and the distant howl of a coyote heralded the night.

"What did you think of her?" he asked, reaching for the tall glass of iced tea sitting on a side table. He knew he could rely on Brian for the truth. Johnny really wanted him to get to know Marci, although that would be difficult without blowing his cover.

"She's pretty and seems very nice. I've been dealing primarily with her sister, so I don't really know her," Brian said and then laughed. "Believe me, Sissy Aguirre is a firecracker." He leaned forward as if he was about to share a secret. "Did you know Vince has the hots for her?"

Johnny sat up so abruptly he spilled tea in his lap. "What?"

"Vince met Sissy in Gruene and he's been talking about her ever since."

Whew! Brian meant Sissy, not Marci. "You're kidding."

"Nope."

"Vince's normal chick du jour is hardly old enough to buy a beer."

"Yeah." Brian snorted. "I'm thinking that since he's about to celebrate his big six five he's considering growing up."

"I wouldn't hold my breath on that one."

The two men sank into silence, contemplating their mutual friend and his vagabond lifestyle.

"Um, this is an interesting topic, but we have some business to discuss," Brian said.

"Unfortunately, you're right." Johnny had been ignoring the bread-and-butter part of his life.

"We have to begin organizing your next tour. We only have a year to get it planned. So, if it's okay with you, I'll start booking some sites."

"Definitely." Touring was not one of Johnny's favorite things to do, primarily because he hated to leave Randy. But next year, his son would be at college, so a tour might be the perfect way to ease into an empty nest.

"And it's time to get back to Nashville."

"I agree. We also need to think about another CD. But I'd like to wait a couple of months on that one." Johnny paused and then broached a different subject. "You're privy to all my secrets."

"Yep. That's why you're so rich. I keep your life in order."

Although Brian was boasting, he truly did keep everything in Johnny's life running like a well-oiled machine.

"So I thought I'd better let you know I want to have a relationship with Marci Hamilton. And I intend to make my business plans based on that."

Brian's look of amazement was priceless.

"Bet you never thought you'd hear me say that, did you?"

His business manager quickly regained his composure. "Not in a million years. Are you sure?"

"Yes, I'm absolutely positive." And when J. W. "Johnny" Watson made up his mind about something, it was a 99-percent done deal.

"What are you planning to do when she learns who you really are?" Brian asked. "Believe me, and I have a wife who'll back me up on this, women do *not* like to be deceived." He shook his head to emphasize the point. "And my friend, this is the granddaddy of all deceptions. I promise she will not be a happy camper when she finds out."

Johnny was aware of that, but he didn't quite know what to do about it. At the moment he enjoyed feeling like a teenager with his first love, and he didn't want reality to muck that up.

And speaking of reality… It came to the forefront when Brian told him about his ex-wife's latest antics.

"Marina called Randy today and asked him to go on the book tour with her."

"*What?*" Johnny jumped up and stalked to the end of the patio. "That bitch."

What had ever possessed him to get involved with her? "How'd you find out?" Johnny asked.

"Randy came by the house to talk to me about it."

Johnny was almost afraid to ask what Randy had decided to do. "So?"

"He told her no, but in a nice way."

That was a relief. "I wonder whether I should go back to Bella Vista for a while," Johnny muttered.

"Why would you want to do that?" Brian asked.

"To check in with Randy and make sure Maria's been feeding him."

"Bad idea. First of all, Maria has been your house-keeper and his surrogate mom for years, so of course she's feeding him. Plus, he's perfectly capable of making his own peanut butter sandwich. He *is* eighteen, and you remember his reaction when you wanted to get him a nanny. He about freaked." Brian laughed.

"Yeah, but—" Johnny started to protest but was cut short.

"If you hightail it home, he's going to know we've been talking, and I don't think that would go over well."

Johnny plopped down on his chair. "So what do you suggest?"

"Call Randy and ask him to come up here for the weekend. It's a win-win situation. You can spend some quality time with your son, and he can get some co-pilot hours in your Gulfstream."

Johnny grinned. "That sounds like it might be workable. I could even introduce him to Marci."

"Now you've got it. I'm sure I don't have to warn you, though, that he has a busy social schedule with life-guarding and dating and all that normal teenage stuff, so you'd better get on asking him."

"Right."

"DO YOU HAVE another date with your big handsome cowboy?" Sissy asked as she lounged on Marci's bed like she owned it. "What are you planning to wear? It needs to be sensual without being too obvious and sexy without being trashy."

Sissy, who happened to be wearing a tight white T-shirt with Jerry Garcia's picture emblazoned on the front, was probably the last person qualified to dispense fashion tips.

"So you don't think my black leather bustier is appropriate?"

Sissy threw a pillow at her. "I'm trying to help."

"Save it for someone who needs it," Marci said as she grabbed the pillow in midflight. "He said jeans." She did a half turn to check out her derrière. "Do they make my butt look fat?"

"Puleeze!"

Marci wasn't convinced, so she continued to rummage through the closet and eventually came up with her favorite white capris.

While she'd been agonizing over the jeans/capris situation, Sissy had wandered off and then reappeared carrying an off-the-shoulder blue blouse.

"Here, this will be fabulous on you. It'll match your eyes."

Marci was touched. That was Sissy's favorite top. "Are you sure?"

"I'm positive." She sat down on the bed. "This man is the one for you, and if I can do anything to help, I'm ready and able."

Marci joined her sister. "I don't know. He's younger than I am."

"How old is he? As far as I'm concerned if he recognizes Buddy Holly and the Beach Boys, he's fair game."

"Somewhere in the neighborhood of fifty-seven, fifty-eight."

Sissy threw her hands in the air. "No big deal. Chronologically speaking, you've got him by a couple of years. Everyone knows men die younger than women."

Marci laughed at her sister's twist of logic. "And that's not the biggest problem."

"Let me guess. Bill."

"Yep, Bill. The last time I had a boyfriend, he turned out to be…well, a killer. It makes me wonder about my taste in men."

Sissy shrugged. "I liked Bill and I suspect that deep down he's a good guy, felonious activities notwithstanding."

"Yeah, I thought he was nice, too. But Lolly feels the situation made me commitment-phobic, and I have to agree with her."

"You need to forget about that and give your handsome cowboy a chance. That's my last word on the subject," Sissy proclaimed as she pranced out of the room.

Her sister was right. Johnny was sexy, fun and downright nice. Was that enough? *Oh, yeah.* If Marci didn't watch out, she might fall head over heels in love with the guy. But she wasn't ready to brave any more heartache. There were other things in life besides chemistry, she told herself, grabbing the blouse.

But as Sissy liked to say, it didn't hurt to look your best.

JOHNNY HAD DECIDED to take Marci to his favorite Mexican restaurant in Kerrville. Not only was the food delicious, the owners were old friends who were very prudent.

After his talk with Brian, Johnny was experiencing a major twinge of guilt. He was tempted to tell her the truth. Tempted, but he hadn't quite reached that point.

"I hope you like Mexican food." He hadn't asked what kind of food she preferred and for all he knew she was allergic to tortillas or chilis.

"I love it."

That was good. "Mama's Mexiteria isn't fancy but the food makes up for the ambiance."

"That's my favorite type of place," Marci said as she settled in the pickup's cracked plastic seat.

"You're so beautiful tonight. Not that you don't always look great, but that blue is the exact color of your eyes." If he didn't think he'd get a concussion, he'd bang his head against the steering wheel. Damn—he sounded like a babbling idiot.

"Thank you." It looked suspiciously as if her quirky smile was about to turn into a belly laugh.

"I have a confession to make." He glanced over so he could see her eyes. "I'm a bit rusty in the dating department, so I'd like you to forgive anything stupid I might say."

"Of course. I'm pretty rusty myself." Marci paused for a moment. "Why don't you date?"

Johnny's attention was back on the road. "I spend most of my time at work or with my teenage son."

"Randy?"

Johnny smiled. "Yeah. Did I tell you he just graduated from high school, and he's the pride of my life?"

She smiled. "You did mention it once or twice, but you didn't tell me where he is right now."

"He's back at the ranch. I'm going to invite him up for a couple of days. I'd love for you to meet him," he added.

So Johnny had a teenage son and she had a teenage grandson. Hmm.

Marci was still pondering their age difference when he pulled into a strip center located on the outskirts of Kerrville. The small restaurant was sandwiched between a Tai Kwan Do studio and a used bookstore. It certainly wasn't the ritziest shopping area in town.

He came around to the passenger door to help her out and didn't relinquish her hand as they strolled into the restaurant.

"Hey, Johnny." A rotund dark-haired man rushed across the small lobby and clapped him on the back. "Good to see you."

"Good to see you, too," Johnny said and turned to Marci. "Marci, this is Paulie and his wife, Benita." He indicated an equally round woman who was rushing across to join the group.

"Johnny!" Benita enveloped him in a hug. "I have a private place all ready for you."

"Great. I told Marci what a terrific cook you are."

The woman beamed at the compliment and led them to an alcove at the back of the restaurant. "I just made *carne asada*." She handed them menus, then kissed the ends of her fingers. "It's *magnifico*."

"Just the thought of *carne asada* makes my mouth water," Johnny said, "but why don't you give us a few minutes so Marci can look at the menu?"

"No, that's okay," Marci said as she handed back the menu, "I love *carne asada* and I'll also have a Corona."

"Make that two," Johnny agreed and waited until Benita left before he took Marci's hand.

"Tell me more about your son." She wanted to hear more about Randy—plus, she was interested in the status of Randy's mother, aka Johnny's wife, girlfriend, whatever.

Like any proud father who's been given the green light to brag, Johnny filled her in on his progeny's school success, athletic abilities and plans for college.

The man was darling when he boasted about Randy's accomplishments. He was in the middle of reliving a particularly memorable football game when Benita arrived with their food.

"The plates are very hot, so be extra careful." Benita instructed as she placed two steaming platters on the table. "Enjoy," she said, patting Johnny on the shoulder before she strolled off.

"They like you. You must be a good customer."

"I come by a lot when I'm in the Hill Country," Johnny said.

Marci was tempted to veer off onto that topic, but she was even more curious about Randy's mother. "What happened to Randy's mother?"

His look turned stormy, leading Marci to believe she'd ventured into a forbidden area. "Never mind," she said.

"No, it's okay." He shrugged, apparently deciding what to tell her.

"I'm divorced and it was nasty," he admitted. "Her name is Marina. I had a good life going when I met her, but looking back, I think I was getting panicked about not having a family. I divorced her when I realized we were making each other miserable. We've been divorced about ten years." He shrugged again and dipped a chip in the salsa. "I hate to bad-mouth her, but she's obsessive, and right now she's making my life a living hell. I just found out she's trying to drag Randy into one of our disputes."

"That's terrible."

He sighed. "Let's talk about something else. How's your dinner?"

"It's great." And it really was some of the best Mexican food she'd ever had.

"After we eat would you like to go for a drive? I want to take you to La Montana to show you the most beautiful view of the Guadalupe Valley around."

"Is that where you're staying?"

"Uh, huh."

"I'd love to see it. I should get back to the inn fairly early, though. The Nashville Network is doing some filming in the morning." She laughed. "And believe me, I need my beauty sleep."

AFTER DINNER THEY DROVE into the hills and turned onto a winding gravel road.

"Where precisely are we going?" she asked, even though deep down she knew she could trust him. But, and this was a big but, she hadn't known him all that long and she hadn't seen any civilization in quite a while.

Johnny hooked an arm negligently over the steering wheel. "I'm taking you to my friend's house. It's one of the prettiest places in the Hill Country." He took a cell phone from his pocket and passed it to her. "Why don't you call your sister and tell her where we are and what we're doing? I'll give you the street names."

Great, now he was clairvoyant.

"Please, it would make me feel better," he said.

"Okay. I do trust you, Johnny."

"I know you do," he said as he drove onto a paved road bracketed by two stone pillars.

Although they'd driven consistently uphill, Marci

wasn't prepared for the house and the vista she encountered when they pulled into a clearing.

"This is La Montana? And your friend owns it?" she asked, in awe of the gorgeous home perched on the edge of the valley.

"Yes to both." He'd already opened his door when she came out with the next question.

"Are you *sure* your friend won't mind you having company?"

"I'm positive."

Marci knew it was presumptuous and more than a bit rude, but she had to ask. "How do you know this guy?"

"We're old friends. He works in Nashville."

The house was a beautiful multilevel structure constructed of a combination of river stone and cedar. And the price tag had to be in the multimillions.

"He must have a huge electric bill." The entire compound featured muted lighting.

"It's a security precaution."

"Oh." The place was so isolated they probably needed additional safety measures. "Are those the guest houses?" Marci indicated several small outbuildings made of the same cedar and stone as the main house. That had to be where Johnny was staying.

"Two of them are guest houses. The largest one is the caretaker's place." Johnny had taken her hand and was leading her down a cobblestone path to the back of the house. "Let's go to the patio where you can see the valley." Marci hoped the caretaker wouldn't take umbrage at his plan.

The setting sun painted the valley in a palette of vivid oranges, reds and yellows.

"Oh, my God, this is beautiful!" Marci exclaimed as

she stood on the rim of the patio watching the sun sink beyond the hills in a halo of molten fire.

"It is wonderful," Johnny agreed. He was standing so close she could smell his wonderful scent—a tantalizing combination of fresh laundry with a hint of citrus.

"Would you like a drink? We have about anything you could want."

"A glass of white wine sounds great, if you don't think your host will mind."

"I know he won't," Johnny said as he went to the bar.

Marci had already settled in one of the comfy chairs when he returned with a crystal flute.

"I hope champagne is okay."

It only took a mention of champagne for Marci to feel the giggles coming on.

"To us." Johnny clinked their glasses in a toast before he sat in the adjacent chair.

"Is there an 'us'?" Marci wasn't sure why she felt compelled to ask the question. Was it really possible to be part of a couple—at her age?

"Yes, ma'am. I hope so."

Much to Marci's surprise...and delight, Johnny coaxed her into his chair. He started with a soft invitational kiss on her neck, then proceeded to a brush of lips across her cheek and a foray to the corner of her mouth. When she put her arms around his neck, he deepened the kiss until it became the kiss of her dreams.

Chapter Thirteen

Marci was still reeling from her evening with Johnny. He made her feel sexy, young and wow! Unfortunately, the cook-off gig was about to get hectic, so for the moment she'd do a Scarlett and ponder it later.

"Are you ready to go?" Sissy called from the living room of their suite. "What did you decide to wear?"

Today was the day the TV folks were planning to film personal vignettes of all the contestants. "I have on my red boots, a denim skirt and the lacy Victorian blouse you hate."

Marci heard an eloquent grunt before Sissy appeared in the door. "Tell me you're not going on TV looking like a refugee from a Jane Austen novel." She did a pirouette to show off a sequined T-shirt. "You need to get glamorous. We're about to be stars."

"I don't want to be glamorous. In fact, I don't even want to be doing this," Marci announced as she marched out the front door. "So get a move on before I change my mind and leave you holding the bag."

THE PREPARATIONS for the weekend festivities were in full swing as the sisters turned into the minuscule parking lot adjacent to the dance hall. Luckenbach. What could you say about Luckenbach, where everybody's somebody? It was Texas's answer to Nashville—a schizophrenic mix of world-class music and an environment rich in cowboy hats and slow-talking good ol' boys.

"Should I take my hair down?" Marci asked, tugging the clip out of her hair. Up, down, ponytail—jeeze, what was wrong with her? She wasn't usually *that* indecisive.

"Leave it down, it looks fine," Sissy said as she pulled the T-Bird up next to the row of Porta-Potties.

"Great parking spot."

"Give me a break," Sissy muttered. She jumped from the convertible and slammed the door so hard, Marci's teeth rattled.

What was *her* problem? The woman was older than dirt so she couldn't be PMSing. It probably had something to do with Harvey. But what? Marci followed Sissy to the tent where the television crews had their cameras rolling.

All things considered, Sissy and Marci's fifteen minutes of TV fame went fairly well. Marci managed to get through the ordeal without breaking into a visible cold sweat, while Sissy, on the other hand, proved to be a natural born performer.

"Would you take a gander at that…that bimbo," Sissy commented when the sisters returned to their booth. She was referring to Idabelle Cornell, a big-haired, blowsy blonde who owned a truck stop restaurant in the Panhandle. She also happened to be one of their fiercest rivals.

"Good Lord, that chick's a camera hog. Plus, she has the mouth of a longshoreman. And," Sissy paused to shoot her adversary one of her best "drop dead" glares. "I think she tries to steal recipes."

"Are you serious?"

"Yep, just watch what she does after the film crew packs up for the day."

Sure enough, when the camera was gone, she eased over to her neighbor's table and riffled though a recipe box.

"I'll be!" Marci exclaimed.

"I knew it. Good thing I have Mama's recipe memorized."

"She's headed this way," Marci said.

Sissy put on her "take no prisoners" face. Oh, man, Marci could see trouble coming.

"Idabelle." Sissy was wearing the dreaded saccharine smile that always preceded a lethal strike. "What can I do for you?"

"Well, hon…" Idabelle snapped her gum. "Just wondered if I could borrow some cayenne?"

"I'm sorry we don't have any—nor do we have a recipe we want to share."

Big oops! Idabelle's face turned an alarming shade of red. "What do you mean?"

Never one to back away from a fight, Sissy retaliated with the truth. "I mean we've been watching you pilfer other people's recipes."

"How dare you, you debutante…" Idabelle looked like she was about to jump over the table and throttle Sissy.

Enough was enough. Marci puffed up to her full five foot ten inches and assumed her chilliest duchess demeanor. Smart people didn't mess with the duchess. "Mrs. Cornell, I'm positive you don't want to do that." Her softly made comment contained enough ice to flash-freeze the woman's ire.

"And please don't bother us again."

Idabelle huffed something indistinguishable before she stalked away.

Marci felt her knees turn to jelly when someone started clapping.

"Well done," Johnny said as he gave her an ovation. He was standing at the rear of the tent and had apparently heard every word of the confrontation. He'd also returned to what she now considered his sunglasses mode.

Marci barely resisted the urge to fall into his arms and let him take care of everything.

That thought was cut short when Sissy spoke. "I guess I pissed her off," she admitted rather sheepishly.

"You sure did! What were you thinking? She's a good thirty pounds heavier than you are and could've beaten the stuffin' out of you." Marci wanted to yell at her sister, but that was the wrong approach. She took a deep breath, as much to give Sissy some calming-down time as to slow her own heart rate. "So let's stay away from her."

Before Sissy could answer, Vince McDowell strolled over.

"What's happenin'? That gal was as mad as an old wet hen when she stomped out of here."

"Nothing," Sissy piped up. "And how are you, Mr. McDowell?"

Apparently she'd recovered from her Idabelle experience.

"Call me Vinnie."

"Vinnie?" Johnny chortled.

"Yeah, *Vinnie*. And what's it to you, *Johnny?*"

Johnny raised his hands in surrender. "Absolutely nothing, Vinnie."

"Have you guys known each other long?" Marci asked.

In unison Johnny answered "no" and Vince said "forever."

"Hmm," Marci said. "Let's try something a little less complicated. How long has Johnny worked for you?" she asked Vince.

"Umm. Well, umm." Vince sidled over next to Sissy. "Darlin', that's a nice shirt."

Marci's years of teaching elementary school had been invaluable in her ability to recognize a stall—and Vince had just accomplished a major league delay.

She was spared the headache of trying to figure it out when she heard a squeal and a familiar teenage voice.

"Mee Maw! We're here."

She glared at Johnny and Vince. "You've been saved by the blondes. I will figure out what's going on," she warned, "and don't you doubt it for a minute."

"Miss Sissy, Miss Marci." Vince tipped his hat to the ladies. "It's been delightful, but I think I'll take my leave now."

"I'm coming, too." Johnny turned to Marci. "I'll talk to you later."

"Okay." She was tempted to say more, but Amanda was jumping up and down demanding her attention, so she ended it simply with, "later."

"Sweetie." Marci opened her arms to give her granddaughter a hug. "And Leslie." She hugged Amanda's best friend and constant companion. "Where's your mama?"

"She and Daddy are putting the twins in their stroller."

"Did Bren come with you?"

Amanda resorted to her newly learned teenage vocabulary. "Like, duh, are you kidding? He's too cool to go places with us."

Marci remembered a time when she thought she was too "cool" to be seen with her parents.

"Hi, Mama, Aunt Sissy." Lolly pushed the stroller while Christian toted several diaper bags.

"Hi, honey." Marci hugged her daughter and then turned her attention to Christian. "I didn't think you guys were coming until tomorrow."

"I was able to take off a day early, so we decided to drive on up." He set the bags on the floor and gave her a hug.

Marci was tempted to breathe a sigh of relief that Johnny and Vince had left. But why was she nervous about Johnny meeting her family? This was nothing more than a summer romance.

Wait—a romance denoted something serious, and this was simply a summer flirtation.

Wasn't it?

Chapter Fourteen

The twins were nestled in their portable bassinette, and Amanda and Leslie were in the adjoining motel room doing what thirteen-year-old girls do—an activity that involved a lot of giggling.

Christian was relaxing on one of the double beds. "I suspect there's something fishy about this Johnny guy," he said. "What do you think?"

Lolly cuddled up next to him. "Although I haven't actually met him, from what Aunt Sissy says, I have to agree. What do you suggest we do?"

"If it's all right with you, I thought I'd get C.J. to come up and sniff him out. He has the best nose in law enforcement."

C.J. was Sheriff C. J. Baker, Christian's best friend and his former partner in the narcotics division.

"Sissy says he keeps making goo-goo eyes at my mother. Plus, he never takes his sunglasses off."

Christian couldn't keep from laughing at his wife's tone of voice.

"Yep," he said as he flipped open his cell phone and punched in C.J.'s number.

"Baker here and it had better be good," C.J. answered.

"Hey, partner. I have a favor to ask. What are you guys doing in the morning?"

Christian heard him repeat the question to Olivia, his wife and Lolly's best friend. He also heard the responding laugh.

"Besides that."

"What do you need?"

Christian knew C.J. would be game for almost anything.

"How would you like to come up to the Hill Country for a barbecue cook-off?"

The long pause was an eloquent answer, but then C.J. asked, "Do you need some help?"

"Yep. I think Mee Maw and some guy she met on a highway are getting involved, and Lolly and I feel there's something squirrelly about him. I want your opinion."

"Just a sec." There was a rustling noise as C.J. talked to Olivia.

"We can be there by noon. Does that work?"

"Hey, that's great. Thanks a million. I owe you one." He closed the phone and rolled over to go nose-to-nose with his wife. "C.J. has one of the best memories around. If our boy's ever had his face on a wanted poster, the sheriff will remember it.

"Fantastic," Lolly murmured as she unfastened the top button of his shirt.

THE COOK-OFF WAS in full swing and the crowds were huge. "Can you believe how many people are here?" Lolly asked. They were strolling to the creek to find a quiet spot for the twins to nap.

Christian set up their portable crib and spread a blanket in the shade of a live oak. "It's nice here." He'd just made himself comfortable when his phone rang. It was C.J. calling to find out where they were.

"It'll take us a few minutes to get there. We had to park out in the north forty."

Ten minutes later, Lolly saw Fang, Olivia and C.J.'s pooch. Fang was white, frou-frou and convinced he was a Rotweiler. He pranced up to the blanket and gave Christian a sloppy kiss.

"Can't you teach him not to do that?" Christian complained, wiping off his face.

"Nope," C.J. said. He and Olivia joined the Delacroix clan on the blanket. Olivia and Lolly started chatting while the guys devised a "get the scoop on Johnny Walker" scheme. They came up with a plan to do some male bonding over a couple of beers. Original—nope. Workable—you bet.

"Lolly, can you get your mom to introduce us to Johnny without arousing her suspicions?" Christian asked after he'd filled the ladies in on their idea.

"I'd be surprised if he wasn't standing there right now. Give me your phone and I'll call her." Lolly talked to her mother for a few minutes and then hung up. "He's at the cook-off tent. I told her you guys are bored and want to meet Harv and this Johnny guy for a drink. Mama said she'll make sure they stick around until you get there. I didn't tell her what you're really up to. She won't be happy with any of us if she finds out. So, you play nice or you'll have to answer to us." Lolly looked to Olivia for affirmation.

"Us, not play nice?" C.J. said in mock astonishment and leaned down to engage his wife in a "we're newlyweds" kiss. "Sweetheart, you know I'm *always* charmin'."

"Unfortunately you're right," Olivia agreed wryly.

"Go." She made shooing motions with her hands. Fang jumped onto her lap and bathed her face in puppy kisses.

"Damn, that dog gets half my lovin'," C.J. groused, prompting his friends to break into a belly laugh.

As C.J. AND Christian strolled to the tent, they agreed on a strategy—they'd have a couple of Shiner Bocks, talk a little sports and then slip in a hint about "wants and warrants." That was about as subtle as two macho lawmen could manage.

"Mee Maw, Aunt Sissy, how're my two best girls?" C.J. gave each of the ladies a hug.

"Harvey, come see who's here," Sissy commanded.

The judges had finished their tasting and most of the crowd was gone, so the contestants were packing their cooking utensils. Harvey was cleaning his portable BBQ pit, but he made time to say "hey."

"Harv, old boy, how are the ladies treating you?" C.J. asked. Both he and Christian felt sorry for Harvey. They couldn't in their wildest dreams imagine traipsing all over Texas hauling that piece-of-crap barbecue pit behind their rig.

"Wanna go for a beer?" Christian suggested.

"Sure," Harvey agreed faster than a rattler could strike. "And let me introduce you to someone. Johnny, come here, I want you to meet some of Port Serenity's finest."

Harvey grabbed a towel and a bottle of hand wash to do a vigorous scrubbing. "Marci told you Johnny's been a big help to us, didn't she?"

"She certainly did," Christian said as Johnny joined Harvey in the hand-washing ritual.

"Johnny, this first dude is Lt. Christian Delacroix. He's Marci's son-in-law and he's a big dog in the Narcotics services of the Highway Patrol. And this is C. J. Baker. He's like one of Marci's kids—and he's our sheriff. C.J., this here's Johnny Walker." Harvey introduced the two men.

"Johnny Walker?" C.J. asked with a chuckle.

"Yeah, I know. My daddy had quite a sense of humor. Glad to meet you, Sheriff, Lieutenant," Johnny said as he toweled his hand and responded in true Texas fashion.

Christian noticed that C.J. started to extend his own hand and paused when Johnny spoke. Even more ominously, C.J. took off his own sunglasses for a better look.

Uh, oh. This had the makings of a picture on the post office wall.

"Well, I'll be…" C.J. snapped his mouth shut before he finished his sentence. "Glad to meet you," he said, then vigorously shook the man's hand.

Now what? Christian suspected his friend was privy to some information he wasn't.

"How about going over to the dance hall with us?" The way C.J. asked the question, it was more of an order than an invitation. And from the look on his face, Johnny apparently understood that, too.

"Sure."

Smart man.

Although the band was playing and there was a crowd on the dance floor doing the Texas two-step, they were able to find a reasonably quiet table in the corner.

"Harvey, would you mind going to get the beers?" Christian asked. Harvey wasn't any slouch in the brains department and more than likely realized something was going on.

"Will do. It might take me a while."

"No problem," Christian assured him.

As soon as Harvey disappeared, C.J. spoke. "Did you really think this—" he made a waving motion with his hand "—disguise would fool anyone?" He ended his question with a chuckle.

Christian hated being out of the loop. What was going on?

Johnny took off his sunglasses and smiled. "It's worked so far, although I did have to resort to a few bribes and threats."

C.J. laughed, and this time it came straight from his belly. "You are *so* busted." He turned to Christian. "I'd like to introduce you to Mr. J. W. Watson, the J. W. Watson of Nashville fame."

Chapter Fifteen

It was a few seconds before C.J.'s announcement registered, and when it did Christian was rendered speechless—something that didn't happen often.

C.J. took advantage of the silence. "So, should I call you Mr. Watson or will Johnny do?"

"Johnny's fine." He removed his baseball cap and set it next to the sunglasses.

"Okay, Johnny. Nice to meet you. It's not every day I get to have a beer with someone famous. I guess the big question is what type of scam is this?"

Before Johnny could begin an explanation, Christian regained his ability to speak.

"Wait just a minute!" He frowned at his best friend. "Why are you two sittin' here kibbutzin' like old pals when this guy—" Christian glared at the singer "—is pulling some hanky-panky with my mother-in-law?" He lapsed into the lethal tone of voice that used to send drug lords scampering for cover.

"Hold it." Johnny raised his hands in surrender, but didn't back down. "I can explain everything."

"Damned straight you're gonna explain." Christian was on the verge of exploding.

"It's like this. I met Marci accidentally when the ladies got lost on their way to New Braunfels. They thought I was a cowboy and I didn't disabuse them of that notion. I still can't figure out what happened when I met her, it was…like I got zapped. Good God, my skin was clammy and my pulse started to race! Damned if I didn't think I was having a heart attack. Needless to say, I had to get to know her better."

Out of the corner of his eye, Christian noticed Harvey heading in their direction with an armload of beers. Until he ferreted out exactly what was going on, the fewer people who were in on this secret, the better. He caught Harvey's eye and waved him off. A cold brew would have to wait.

"Why?"

Johnny looked puzzled for a moment. "Why what?"

"Why would you want to get to know Marci? With you being rich and famous and all, I wouldn't've thought she'd be your type. I love her and she's great. But she *is* a retired kindergarten teacher."

Johnny leaned forward as if to confide in them. "You're seeing her through different eyes than I am. Not every man over the age of fifty-five is interested in a blond twenty-year-old bimbo." Johnny was on a roll and didn't seem inclined to stop. "I'm enthralled by Marci. To me she's beautiful, smart, funny and she has a heart the size of Texas. What more could a man want?"

Christian and C.J. glanced at each other. Their wives fit that description to a T, and they were very happy men.

"So if this isn't a con for your recreation, how do you see it playing out?" C.J. asked the question, beating Christian by only a second.

"She's gonna be mad when she discovers you've

been deceiving her." That comment came from Christian.

"I'm afraid you're right," Johnny conceded. "I just wanted to get to know her without all the extra stuff messing things up. Now I'm afraid I have a huge problem."

"Sure enough," Christian said with conviction.

C.J. grinned.

OH, BOY. He was in a mess of trouble! Despite the fact that these two lawmen had probably considered beating the crap out of him, Johnny liked them. It must've had something to do with their protective attitude toward Marci.

"I...uh, I need your help," Johnny admitted. He hoped they could come up with a miraculous parting-of-the-Red-Sea solution to his problem. More than likely, it *would* take heavenly intervention to salvage this situation.

The woman he loved— Good Lord, there was that *L* word again—was gonna kill him when she learned about his deception.

"Well, partner, what do you think?" C.J. asked his friend. "Should we help him or should we let him stew in his own juices?"

"I'm leaning toward letting him dig himself out of this one," Christian said, then grinned. "Naw, let's help him. But we've got to handle it right or our wives will have our butts."

"Ain't that the truth," C.J. concurred.

"What can we do?" Christian asked Johnny.

"I don't know." Praise God, they were willing to help him. But help him do what? He was fresh out of ideas.

Christian was the first to break the silence. "You'd better not make her unhappy, 'cause if you do I might have to use you for target practice."

Johnny laughed, although he wasn't entirely convinced the man was kidding. "I'm as serious as I've ever been about a woman."

"Serious as in marriage?" Christian obviously wasn't about to drop the subject.

That was a good question. Johnny's only foray into matrimonial bliss had turned out to be anything but blissful. His gut, however, was telling him that the situation would be very different with Marci.

"Maybe." He rubbed a hand over his eyes, thinking about life with the tall blonde.

It was what they both needed. "I can't say for sure that's how this'll all work out. I mean, she's gonna be *really* mad, and she can be stubborn. I'm not positive I can talk her into getting married."

Johnny's heart sank when the two men agreed with him. He was halfway hoping they'd tell him he was full of it.

Okay, it would be a challenge, but challenges were nothing new. First, he needed to see Randy. After that, he wanted to spirit Marci off to someplace private. La Montana wasn't an option; she'd never buy his story that his "friend" had given him a key to the front door. Then it hit him—an idea that would allow him to do two things at once.

"How about this? I'll invite Marci to San Antonio. Vince has a house in the King William District and I have an open invitation to use it. I think a little privacy is in order. We can go tomorrow." That also worked perfectly into Johnny's plan to talk to Randy.

"You guys can fill your wives in on what's happening and make yourselves scarce. Marci won't leave if you're still here. I also think you should hide this from Sissy. Anything she knows, Marci knows."

Christian winked at C.J. "This ought to be a kick in the head."

C.J. tipped his chair back and grinned. "If we're lucky, we can keep the lynch mob, aka our wives, off your tail for a few days. But you'd better do this right, because Miss Marci can be mighty formidable. Man, I'd hate to be in your boots."

Johnny glanced down at his Nikes. It was time to get back to his boots. "Do you think the girls can hang on to a secret?"

Christian grimaced. "It'll take some persuasion, but I believe I can talk Lolly into giving you a little time. Not much, mind you, but some. And let me warn you, you really don't want to see her mad. So don't mess this up."

"Warning heeded. So, you guys are gonna talk to your wives, and my assignment is to convince Marci to go to San Antonio with me. Right?"

"Right," Christian said. "And I'd appreciate it if you kept us informed."

That would be easy enough, Johnny thought as they traded cell phone numbers. If he really got into trouble, he'd simply call his two newest friends.

"Now that's settled, let's get Harv over here before he drinks all the beer," C.J. suggested, catching Harvey's eye.

"I'll leave you to it and go find Marci," Johnny said.

If he pulled this off, he'd be the luckiest guy in the world. If he didn't…well, he couldn't afford to fail. Not when he was dealing with the rest of his life.

Chapter Sixteen

Randy had said yes readily enough. He'd arrive at Vince's that night. Having a teenage chaperone didn't exactly mesh with a romantic getaway, but sometimes you had to take what you could get.

Johnny's next job was to cajole Marci into taking a little road trip. And as difficult as that assignment might seem, it would be a walk in the park compared to what Christian and C.J. faced in persuading their wives to go home.

Johnny hurried through the tent looking for Marci. When Brian had originally mentioned the cook-off idea, he'd thought *why not*. Now that he'd witnessed the time and effort involved in coordinating a multi-event scenario, plus TV coverage, Johnny was convinced his business manager and staff were miracle workers.

Despite an uncomfortable environment—when the crowds were huge, the TV folks annoying and the heat inside the tent oppressive—Marci had maintained a smile and a prize-winning attitude. What a woman!

Johnny, on the other hand, had been tempted to deck a couple of the flip-flop-wearing tourists—especially when they dissed his ladies' cooking. Thank God this leg of the trip was almost over and only a few hard-core stragglers remained in the tent.

"Hey, darlin'." Johnny slipped up behind Marci and put his arms around her waist. She leaned her head back on his chest and gave a deep sigh.

"We're almost finished. I can't believe we still have two of these things to go."

"Yeah, I hear you," Johnny said as he wiped a drop of sauce from her chin. It took enormous willpower not to lick it off.

"I have a favor to ask," he murmured.

"Sure, anything."

"Anything?" He arched an eyebrow.

"Well, um…"

Johnny took pity on her. "I'd like you to go to San Antonio with me. Randy's going to be at Vince's house and I need to touch base with him."

"Why didn't you say so?" She caressed the side of his cheek. "You know I'd love to meet your son, but my family's here and I can't leave them. That would be rude."

Johnny couldn't tell her he'd solved that problem. Fortunately Sissy scurried up, with Vince and Harvey following behind, so he was spared having to make a response.

"We won! We won this round!" Sissy held up her hands for a congratulatory high five. "We get a ton of points for winning." The sisters squealed as they danced around the booth.

"We won." Marci's grin spread from ear to ear as she did another little jig. "I might be able to get my VW convertible, after all."

"Is that why you're doing this?" Johnny asked.

Marci shrugged, but the grin broke out again. "Pretty much. That and I wanted an adventure."

If he had his druthers, this would end up being the most exciting time of her life….

"Mama, Aunt Sissy." Lolly parted the straggling tourists by using her twin stroller. Christian trailed behind with a sheepish expression on his face.

"Congratulations! They just made the announcement. I think the TV folks are going to be here shortly."

Johnny didn't miss the look she shot him. Yep, she knew what was going down and she wasn't too happy about it. He glanced at the camera crew headed their way and decided to make himself scarce.

WITH A FLURRY of kisses and hugs, Marci waved goodbye to the Delacroix clan and the Baker bunch.

What was their big hurry, anyway? "Where's Johnny?" Marci asked her sister. "He was here a little while ago."

Sissy was busy flirting with Vince, and Harvey was busy scowling. Who could blame him? Big sis could be incredibly annoying.

"The last I saw him, he was moseying off to the creek." Vince provided that bit of information.

"Thanks," Marci said as she wandered out of the tent in search of both Johnny and a cool spot. During the afternoon, she'd transitioned from glowing to sweating like a pig.

Although there were a few die-hard tourists wandering around, most people had departed after Vince's concert. Smart folks—a shower and a cold beer sounded like heaven.

"Hey," she said when she found him sitting in the shade of an ancient pecan tree.

"Hey, yourself," Johnny replied as he pulled her

down to join him on the grass. "Want a cold drink?" he asked as he held up a bottle of water.

"Okay." She took a swig and handed the bottle back to him.

"I talked to Christian as they were packing up to leave. So are you ready to go into the city with me? I promise we'll have a good time." He plastered on a grin. "Even if we've got a chaperone."

"What… Oh, right. Randy will be there."

"How about it?"

"Sure, why not? I have to run back to the inn to pick up some clothes and let Sissy know what I'm doing."

HOW MUCH TROUBLE could they get into with a teenage escort? A lot, if Marci had anything to say about it.

Chapter Seventeen

Johnny had a game plan—a damned good one. Sort of… So why was he sweating bullets? Honesty *was* the best policy, wasn't it? Uh, huh, if you didn't mind getting pummeled, and pummeling wasn't at the top of his wish list. The fact that they were speeding down I-10 might be his only saving grace when he made his confession.

"Marci, I have something I need to tell you."

"What—? Marci's question was interrupted by the chirp of her cell phone. "Darn," she said as she glanced at the caller ID. "It's the same weird phone call I've been getting for weeks. It's that *out of area* thing again.

"Are you still getting those calls?"

Before answering his question she snapped open the phone. "Hello, hello, stop calling me! I. Am. Not. Amused." She broke the connection and threw the phone into her purse. "That makes me so mad."

Johnny looked at her. She'd gone from smiling to livid in about two point two seconds. Wow. He'd never seen her so…agitated.

"Why didn't you tell me someone is still calling you?" He was trying to maintain a calm he didn't feel.

"Well, um, I'm not *sure*, but I suspect I know who's been phoning me."

So she had secrets, too. "Why don't you tell me about it." For a moment he thought she was about to clam up; then she sighed.

"Last year I started dating a guy I really liked," she began with an embarrassed grin. "I hadn't dated in a very long time. He was everything I wanted in a man. He was smart and funny and loving. Too bad he also turned out to be a murderer."

"A murderer!" Johnny sputtered. Marci had dated a *murderer*.

"Yep, and even better, he ended up on *America's Most Wanted*." She went into a lengthy explanation about Port Serenity's summer of dead drug dealers and the part Bill and his buddies had played in that macabre spectacle.

"I hate to admit I did this, and Lolly would die if she knew I was quite so stupid, but Sissy and I seriously considered meeting him in Guadalajara. Fortunately, we came to our senses and ditched that idea. I didn't really want to know where he was living because I would've had to inform Christian." She frowned. "Bill was a huge mistake, but believe it or not, he's a nice guy. His problem is that he has an incredibly screwed-up sense of ethics."

"No kidding." Johnny was so busy trying to keep from cussing a blue streak he almost missed the next thing she said.

"The reason I think Bill's the one who's been calling me is because one time I heard someone speaking Spanish in the background."

"Have you put a trace on it?"

"No, I'm not sure I want to know if it's him. I did a

poor job of breaking up with him and I'm afraid he didn't quite get the message."

Good God! The woman he loved was being pursued by a murderer. There was that "woman he loved" business again.

"So…" Marci shrugged before she continued. "That, in a nutshell, is why I'm leery of getting involved with anyone."

Johnny spotted a rest area and pulled in. "Let's sit at the picnic table and have a little talk." Driving and discussing murder was even more hazardous than driving and talking on a cell phone.

He could tell she didn't want to resume the discussion; however, she reluctantly agreed so he took her hand and led her to the table.

"I promise *I'm* not a murderer. I've never been in jail. I don't have any wants or warrants. I have a clean driving record."

Unfortunately, he did have a doozy of a secret.

She stared at their joined hands. "Deception is the one thing I'd have a hard time forgiving."

Oooh, boy! Johnny pondered the situation for a few seconds and decided to go for a bit of honesty. Not total honesty—that would have to wait. At least until he figured out *how* to fess up. He didn't want to make St. Peter's acquaintance anytime soon.

"I think I'm falling in love with you." The truth was, he was definitely in love with her—heart-and-soul in love. But with a woman like Marci, slow and easy was the key.

"I don't expect you to say anything. Let's take it one step at a time and see what happens. I'll be around when you're ready, I promise." He emphasized his vow with a gentle brush of their lips. "So let's get going. I'm anxious for you to meet Randy."

TALK ABOUT BEING bowled over. He was falling in love with her—or to be more accurate, he said he *thought* he was falling in love. In love. Whew. Marci mentally fanned herself. What a conundrum. She loved him, yep; it took a lot to confess that, even to herself. But was she ready to trust any man? The Bill debacle had taken a terrible toll on her confidence.

She was still contemplating the situation as they drove through downtown San Antonio. "You didn't tell me where Vince's place is located."

"It's in the King William District."

"That's nice." Marci had heard about the historic area of old homes. "I always meant to drive through there and enjoy the houses."

"You'll like it. Vince's housekeeper is expecting us. Aurora's a great cook."

"You and Vince must be good friends if he's lending you his place."

"I guess you could say that. We go back a long time."

JOHNNY HAD NEVER really discussed anything personal with her. There were a couple of things she did know: where he went to college, that he had a son he loved very much and an ex-wife he didn't care for at all. And she knew that sometimes he worked on a ranch and sometimes he worked for Vince McDowell. All in all, that wasn't much to build a relationship on.

All her questions were momentarily lost when he entered the driveway of an antebellum mansion with wraparound verandas on both levels.

"Holy cow! *This* is Vince's house?" It wasn't a house. It was a freakin' mansion and all she had in her suitcase was a pair of jeans. They dressed for dinner in places like that. Good grief!

"It sure is. I can't wait for you to meet Randy."

Johnny parked next to the carriage house at the rear of the property and escorted her to the back door.

"Aurora is Vince's housekeeper, and she's an old friend of the family. If we're lucky, she'll have something baking. That is, if Randy hasn't already eaten it. Keeping that kid in food is tough."

It was another one of those comments that made Marci wonder about Johnny's financial situation. His car, his clothes, everything led to the impression he was having a hard time, regardless of the fact that he had quite a few wealthy friends.

"Mr. Johnny, I'm so glad you're here." An older woman with skin the color of cappuccino engulfed him in a bear hug.

"Aurora, girlfriend, did you miss me?" He winked at her, eliciting a series of giggles. "This is my friend, Marci Hamilton. Marci, this is Aurora, the best cook in San Antonio."

"You flatter me." The housekeeper affectionately swatted Johnny. "Very nice to meet you, Mrs. Hamilton," she said.

"Please call me Marci."

"Marci." The housekeeper nodded, then turned to Johnny.

"Randy's in the den watching some silly sports. Baseball, football, who knows." She threw up her hands in good-natured surrender. "He probably didn't hear you come in, so shoo, go find your boy. Marci, I'll fix us a cup of tea and we'll sit down for a nice chat."

Marci could tell that Johnny wanted a private conversation with his son and Aurora was acting as a facilitator.

"That would be lovely. Is there anything I can do?"

"Not a thing. Sit, sit, I have some chocolate chip cookies right out of the oven."

Who could argue with that?

Aurora and Marci had a wonderful grandma-to-grandma discussion of everything from bare midriffs on beer bellies to teenage gangs, and gave a big thumbs-down to both.

JOHNNY HEARD the laughter before he and Randy made it to the kitchen.

"What are my two best girls up to?" he asked as he planted a kiss on top of Marci's head.

The women answered in unison. "Nothing."

Yeah, right, and he had some swamp land for sale. "Marci, I want you to meet Randy." He put an arm around his son's shoulders.

"Glad to meet you, Mrs. Hamilton."

God bless Randy, he was proud of the kid. He knew his manners and practiced them.

Instead of shaking the teen's hand, Marci gave him a hug. Undoubtedly that shocked him; Marina wasn't the warm, demonstrative type and in his young life, motherly hugs had been few and far between.

"I'm Marci, okay?"

"Randy has a hankerin' for dinner at Mi Tierra." Johnny was referring to a well-known Mexican restaurant at El Mercado, an area that had originally been a farmer's market, but was now a quaint shopping area featuring Mexican products and restaurants.

"That sounds fantastic," Marci said. El Mercado was another place she'd always wanted to visit.

"Aurora, you're included in the invitation."

"Aw, Mr. Johnny, that's nice, but I think I'll go visit my grandbabies."

Randy had fortunately parked his Dodge Hemi in the garage, since Johnny had decided to maintain the "poor boy" façade, at least for the time being.

"I'll drive," he said, but he didn't miss his son's arched brow. When Johnny had explained the situation, Randy had immediately jumped aboard the truth train. In typical teenage fashion he'd gone straight to the heart of the matter with a succinct "You are in hot water" comment.

THEY ALL SQUEEZED into the cab of the battered pickup. Marci sat in the middle and felt like she was being wrapped in a testosterone burrito. Not bad, not bad at all.

The market was everything she'd heard and more. And the food at Mi Tierra was delicious beyond description. Marci savored a culinary fiesta of crispy chimichangas, creamy guacamole, homemade tamales and crunchy tacos.

"I think I just gained five pounds," she declared as she studied the large platter she'd almost licked clean.

"Me, too," Johnny muttered.

They had chosen to eat on the patio shaded by colorful umbrellas. A soft breeze kept it from feeling oppressively hot.

"Would you like another margarita?" Johnny asked.

"I want one," Randy piped up with a big grin.

"In your dreams, kid." Johnny grinned back.

It was a magical evening. They talked, and laughed, and Marci discovered that Randy was a special kid. He was charming and charismatic. Add that to good looks courtesy of his dad and you had a delightful combo. Johnny was justifiably proud of him.

"Let's wander through the market," Johnny suggested.

El Mercado was a replica of a Mexican market. Marci was surrounded by color—piñatas, pottery, tiles, textiles and paper flowers. The reds, yellows, blues and greens made the small aisles resemble a spring garden.

"Would you like a steer skull for your living room wall?" Johnny asked.

"Are you kidding? I'd love one," Marci said, and then broke into laughter. "Actually, it's not as bad as the stuffed snake. That was gross."

LATE THE NEXT AFTERNOON, they drove back to Fredericksburg.

"I had a fantastic time," she told him as he walked her to the inn's front door. "I'm glad you talked me into going. I'm also delighted I got to meet Randy. I enjoyed him so much."

"He enjoyed meeting you, too."

After Marci had gone to bed, Johnny got an earful from his son. He said Marci was terrific and declared that his father was dumber than a hundred head of sheep if he let her get away. In his infinite teenage wisdom he'd insisted that Johnny would lose her if he didn't fess up, PDQ.

The kid was right. Now all Johnny had to do was come up with another game plan. A *foolproof* game plan.

Piece of cake—uh, huh.

Chapter Eighteen

Marci had had a ball during the week in Fredericksburg and Luckenbach—and especially her weekend in San Antonio. It was all because of Johnny. She was afraid she was falling in love. What, oh, what should she do?

"Get a move on it." Sissy swatted her sister as she stumbled out the door with her massive suitcase.

Sometimes their sisterly connection was incredibly inconvenient. It had taken Sissy about half a second to pick up on the fact that love was in the air. It had taken her less than a minute to become a royal pain in the butt—dancing around the suite singing "love is in the air."

"We're going to a rodeo." Sissy pranced back in with her pink Stetson on her head.

Marci reverted to being uppity. "That clashes with your hair." If Sissy didn't quit singing, Marci was gonna have to do something violent, because, yes, darn it, love *was* in the air. And it was making her cranky.

Marci stalked out to the convertible and demanded the keys, hoping that mindless driving would clear her head. Since for most of the trip to the Ozona rodeo they'd be on Interstate 10, at least she didn't have to worry about getting lost.

For some reason—heaven only knew what—Johnny had hitched a ride with Harvey in the Suburban. His piece-of-crap truck had probably died of extreme old age.

"I have to pee," Sissy announced.

"We just got on the Interstate. Can't you hold it?"

"Nope," she said and squirmed around in the seat. "I had three cups of coffee. So sue me."

"Can you wait for a couple of miles, or do you want to go out there in the poison ivy?" Marci indicated miles and miles of ranch land. "I saw a sign for a rest area two miles ahead."

"I can wait. I'll call Harv and tell him we're stopping."

Why Harvey needed to know that, Marci had no idea.

He and Johnny were already sitting at a picnic table when Marci completed her trip to the ladies' room and joined them.

"What's taking Sissy so long?" Harvey asked and then chuckled. "You don't have to answer. She's primping."

At that very moment Sissy ran up. "Harvey, Harvey come with me." She grabbed his hand and pulled him away from the picnic table.

"What now?" Marci asked, even though her question was obviously rhetorical.

Johnny shrugged quizzically.

"Marci, come here!" The disembodied voice came from the bushes.

"What *are* they doing?"

"Let's go see," Johnny said.

He'd just finished his sentence when Sissy popped out of the vegetation holding a fuzzy and wiggly bundle.

"People make me so mad I can hardly see straight," she muttered. Sissy rarely got eye-popping, knee-knocking mad, but this time she was furious.

"Someone dumped a litter of kittens. A whole litter of babies, plus their mama. Six little ones." She held up a tiny gray fuzz ball. The mother cat twirled around Sissy's legs meowing to beat the band.

"We're gonna take 'em with us," Sissy proclaimed. "The whole bunch of 'em."

Marci was well aware that they couldn't leave the helpless kittens miles from civilization. Those babies would become a coyote snack before the night was over.

Not going to happen!

"So, how do we handle the logistics of our adoption?" Marci asked, ever the practical member of the duo.

"We'll find a box. And Harvey, don't you have an old blanket in the back of the Suburban?"

Harvey and Johnny looked like they'd both rather have a root canal without anesthetic than participate in this dramatic rescue, but Sissy's ex managed a weak nod.

"Sugar, why don't you get it for me while I find a box?" Sissy didn't wait for his answer before she headed toward the Dumpster by the restrooms. She was still carrying the little bundle of fuzz, with mama cat right behind her. Pitiful, tiny cries floated from the bushes.

"We're comin', babies, don't ya worry. We're comin'," Sissy crooned, in full earth-mother mode. She'd save the world if she thought she could, and Marci loved her dearly for that trait.

Before Marci could say "Jack Sprat," Sissy had the feline family comfortably situated in the back of the Suburban. She did it with such aplomb you'd think it wasn't unusual to bop down the freeway with a feline entourage and a Paul Bunyan-size mobile barbecue pit.

Only in Texas!

"I'm going to ride with Harvey to keep an eye on the

babies. Johnny, you go with sister. We'll stop at the next convenience store or truck stop to buy some cat food." Sissy didn't give anyone a chance to object to changing cars or stopping.

Lord, that woman could have coordinated D-Day without batting an eyelash.

"THIS IS WORKING out well," Johnny said as he threw his Stetson in the back seat and stretched out his legs.

He had ditched his baseball hat and shorts and had donned faded jeans and a battered cowboy hat. However, he was maintaining his strange sunglass fetish.

"We have six hours together in a car. What better way to get to know someone than a long road trip?"

"So," Marci said. "Tell me about Marina."

Chapter Nineteen

For almost three hours Johnny filled Marci in on all the important aspects of his life with Marina—the heartache, the disappointment and the ultimate sense of failure. There were a couple of things he neglected to share. Big things—like Marina's book and the fact that she still wore her six-carat diamond engagement ring. He never had understood why she kept that ring. He hoped to God Brian wasn't right about her Fatal Attraction.

While they were having their discussion, they devoured a two-liter bottle of Dr Pepper, a bag of Cheetos and an entire box of powdered doughnuts.

"I hate to mention this, but I need to see a man about a dog," Johnny said, sheepishly reverting to an old Texas saying.

"If you can wait a few minutes, I'm sure the Clampetts in the Suburban will have to make a pit stop. Sissy has the smallest bladder in the state."

"I hear ya."

True to Marci's prediction, Harvey pulled off at the next exit.

A COUPLE OF HOURS and miles and miles of scrub rangeland later, they made a second stop at a scenic overlook.

From the top of the hill, they could see that the elevation suddenly dropped. Spread out before them in the valley below was the town of Ozona.

A true West Texas enclave, Ozona was an oasis in the middle of millions of acres of ranchland. In West Texas if you had a ten-thousand-acre spread, it was considered a good start. If you had a hundred thousand acres you were getting there—especially if the oil-pump jacks were dancing a jig on your property.

Ozona was a Marlboro Man moment in a real-deal cowboy way. It was a place where preschoolers rode like professionals, teenage girls were barrel racers before they got their first training bras, and young men cut their teeth on bucking broncs.

"I'm glad we're finally here," Marci said.

"Towns are few and far between," Johnny responded.

In this part of the world, it wasn't unusual for the next outpost of civilization to be sixty miles away, or for ranch kids to make a hundred-mile daily trip on a big yellow bus.

Johnny had always loved West Texas. Maybe it was the isolation, or perhaps it was the pioneer spirit; whatever it was, folks in towns from Sonora to Fort Davis knew how to take care of themselves. They also took care of each other. This was the home of comfort food—fried okra, homemade mac n' cheese, Jell-O salads with fruit cocktail, chicken-fried steak and peach cobbler.

Johnny had assumed map-reading duties. "Take the first exit off the freeway, go down that road for a mile, and we'll find the motel." Harvey nodded and everyone jumped into their respective cars for the ride into Ozona.

Marci followed the Suburban into the portico of the Best Western. This would be their home for the next week.

"Are you staying here?" Marci asked.

"Nope, I'm going to a friend's house."

She gave him a sideways glance. "You seem to have friends all over the state. Nice friends."

"Yep, I have a few. And they are nice." Marci didn't need to know that he was staying in a mansion—one of many in this town of 3,000—owned by the buddy who'd given him his first financial stake.

"Do you need a ride?"

"That's not necessary. I'll call him and he'll pick me up." Johnny was having second thoughts about not staying at the motel. If he did, he'd have more time with Marci. More time to make sure she loved him, so when she discovered the truth it wouldn't make any difference. And there was no doubt in his mind that she'd eventually realize who he was. He just wanted it to be on his terms.

Time was limited because the Ozona folks knew their country western stars. If he wasn't recognized here, it would fall under the heading of a miracle—and at this point he could use some help from above.

"I'm going in to see if Sissy has our key. Do you want to go with me?" Marci had parked and was about to get out of the car. "You can use the phone in our room."

"I'll call my friend from here." Johnny held up his cell. "But first we have some business to attend to."

Marci looked confused. "What?"

"This." He put his hand on the back of her neck and tugged her gently across the console. Even though he only intended to give her a soft "see you later" kiss, his well-meaning intentions melted like Hershey's candy in a hot car. She smelled like flowers, her skin felt like velvet—and what red-blooded American guy could resist that combination?

When he regained his senses he was shocked that they were necking like a couple of teenagers—in a public parking lot.

The paparazzi would have a field day with that one.

He was deliberately taking his time because Marci always seemed on the verge of scampering off. That *wasn't* on his agenda. However, he was afraid his luck might desert him so he needed to prepare for his big revelation sooner rather than later.

"Oh, boy," he said as he took a deep breath. She was so cute all rumpled and looking well kissed. If he didn't get out of there immediately, he wouldn't be able to leave at all. As it was, he was going to have a hard time walking.

"Why don't you locate Sissy and see how she plans to smuggle the kitties into her room."

"Hmm?"

"Sissy, cats, motel room." He kissed the side of her mouth, the tip of her nose and her forehead. "Do any of those ring a bell?"

It was as if she snapped out of a trance. "That's right, I need to find Sissy."

"I want to take you to dinner. Harrison will lend me a car," Johnny said as he got out and leaned back in the open window. "I'll pick you up at seven. I remember a diner that has food even better than my mama's."

"Seven." The man had more contacts than a Mafia godfather.

Sissy had mama cat and her babies safely stashed away by the time Marci tracked down their room and unloaded her bag.

"Aren't they about the cutest things you've ever seen?" Sissy asked, but didn't wait for an answer before she continued. "Are you getting sick? You look flushed."

"Yes, they're darling," Marci said, picking up a fuzzy calico, "and, no, I'm not getting sick." Not unless raging lust was an illness. Later, much later, she'd bring Sissy up to speed. Their ability to keep secrets from each other was almost nonexistent.

"How was your trip with Johnny?" From anyone else the question would've been innocent. But not Sissy, especially when she wore her all-knowing smirk.

"Fine."

"Just fine?" she asked, watching one of the two white kittens make an awkward attempt to get out of the shallow box.

Marci picked up the kitten as she sat down on the edge of the bed. "We can name this one Frosty." Distracting Sissy was almost impossible, but this time she'd give it a shot.

"You can name it anything you want as long as you're going to keep it."

Marci put the baby in the box again. "I don't need a cat."

"Stop changing the subject. Let's get back on track," Sissy demanded, waggling her fingers in Marci's face. "Now give."

"You're irritating, you know that?"

"It's one of my more endearing qualities, and stop stalling."

Marci fell back on the bed and let the kitten walk on her chest. "I suspect I'm falling in love or lust or something. And it's making me crazy."

"Why?" Sissy asked. She picked up the calico, then sat down with her on the bed. "Johnny is Mr. Stud Muffin and it's obvious he's smitten with you, so what's the problem?"

"The problem is I don't know all that much about him. I've met his son, and he's delightful. But Johnny's so closemouthed about what he does for a living. Ranch worker, roadie—none of it really makes sense. I mean, the guy seems to set his own hours." Marci sat up, placing the kitten on the comforter. "And don't you think it's strange that he has so many rich friends?"

Frowning, Sissy played with the kittens. "Yeah, I have to admit that's rather unusual, especially for a guy who works on a ranch. Plus, it's as if Vince looks up to him. It's Johnny this and Johnny that. What's the deal?"

"I don't know, but I do know that if this one goes south I'm swearing off men for the rest of my life," Marci declared. "I can't take another Bill disaster, not that I think Johnny would ever do anything felonious."

Sissy nodded her concurrence. "And speaking of Bill, have you ever considered that those weird calls might be from him? I can't come up with anyone else who might be doing that sort of thing, although I'm not sure why he would, either."

"I did think of that." Marci hesitated. "But it's strange. The calls stopped for a while and then right after we got back from San Antonio, I got another one. This time it was different. Instead of *out of area* on the caller ID, it said *Private Caller*. And swear to God, there was a gravelly voice that said 'bitch.' Bill would *never* do that."

"No, he wouldn't. The man loved you."

"That's what makes me so sad about the whole mess. And it also gives me second thoughts about getting involved with another guy."

Sissy nodded as she continued to play with the calico. "Let's name this one Shirley."

"Sounds like a good name."

"Why don't we take a spin around town and see the

lay of the land," Sissy suggested. "We'll put the top down and feel like we're seventeen."

"I have to be back around six so I can get a shower. Johnny's taking me to supper."

Sissy broke into an infectious laugh. "You distracted me for a minute there. Don't think that'll happen again. I want the straight skinny on what you've been doing with our tall, dark and handsome cowboy."

THE SPIN THROUGH the small town didn't take long; however, it did present a few surprises. As I-10 meandered almost nine hundred miles east to west through Texas, the topography changed from coastal plains to the rolling green beauty of the Hill Country to the semi-arid scrub brush desolation of far West Texas. Bleak was a charitable description for the scenery they'd encountered before they'd topped the hill and spied the green oasis below.

Ozona was founded in that oasis, near a river. The hardy pioneers had planted trees—live oaks and pecans that grew to provide treasured shade.

"Quaint town," Marci commented. They were driving by a series of impressive buildings dating back to early in the twentieth century.

"Uh, huh," Sissy agreed as she made another circle of the courthouse square. "Let's check out the facilities at the rodeo arena. Harvey told me there's a big convention center where they're holding the cook-off. Thank God we'll be out of that tent and into the air conditioning. Too bad the barbecue pit will be outside."

"Poor Harvey," Marci said and meant that in every sense of the word. It was apparent to everyone, except her sister, that although Harvey might be her ex, he was still madly in love with her. And if Sissy continued to flirt with Vince McDowell, Marci was afraid Harvey would take matters into his own hands.

"I'm going to insist that our booth isn't anywhere near Idabelle Cornell's. She makes my skin crawl," Sissy said as she parked the car under the shade of a large pecan tree.

Marci couldn't agree more. A couple of their competitors had gotten sick during the Luckenbach festivities. Strangely enough, their booths were located on either side of Idabelle's.

"Do you think she did something?" Marci asked.

"It's possible. She's ruthless—and insanely competitive."

"Let's be really careful and not ever leave the booth or the food unattended," Marci said.

"You bet." Sissy paused and shook her fist for emphasis. "And if I find her anywhere near our stuff, I'm gonna bitch slap her into the next county. That ought to put an end to her meanness."

Marci had to laugh at the image. "That's just wonderful. I've always wanted to visit an inmate in the Crockett County Jail. Tell you what, I'll bring a nail file—in lieu of bailing you out."

THERE WAS NOTHING like reliving old times with great friends. Throw in a cold brew and you had it made.

"Wonderful place you have here." Johnny gestured at Harrison Tompkins' mahogany-paneled den. His college roommate's home—read mansion—seemed better suited to a Savannah plantation than the high plains of West Texas.

With his faded jeans, battered boots and a haircut that

looked as if he'd stuck his head in a blender, Harrison was the antithesis of a typical high-powered business-man. Not surprising, since the guy had been into under-statement his entire life.

"Sally said to tell you hey. She's in Dallas shopping with her sister," Harrison said.

"Tell her hi for me. You know, I don't remember the last time I visited you," Johnny admitted. "I'm going to have to make more of an effort."

"Damned straight you are. Come for deer season. I have a great hunting shack out on the ranch."

"Sure," Johnny agreed, although he knew he'd find an excuse not to show. Killing Bambi wasn't his thing.

"Carlton's gonna be here in a few minutes." Harrison was referring to one of their fraternity brothers.

"Good," Johnny said as he sipped his second beer. "I haven't seen him in years. Does he still have that big spread over near Alpine?"

"Yep, he's the oil mogul in this part of the world."

Johnny laughed, shaking his head at that turn of events. When they were in college, Carlton Summerville had considered ketchup one of the major food groups. His frugality was a product of a family that was land rich and cash poor.

"Last I heard, he was married to a Dallas debutante. I had trouble understanding that one. He was such a wild man. He barely knew what to do with one fork, much less three or four."

"Boy, are you in for a shock. The deb is history." Harrison grinned. "And he's a deacon in the Baptist Church."

"No kidding!"

"You'll see. Now, back to you. Not that I'm not glad you're here, but I want to know exactly what you're up to."

Johnny winced at his friend's blunt question. Harrison deserved an explanation, especially since Johnny was relying on him to keep this ruse going.

"Okay, it's like this." He told him everything, and much to his surprise he even found himself using the *L* word.

Harrison's reaction was a long, hard stare followed by a belly laugh.

"Holy crap, you have gotten yourself into it. The Johnny Walker 'I'm never gonna get married again' Watson is in love. Wow!"

"That about covers it. So are ya in?"

"Yep, I surely am. I wouldn't miss it for the world. When am I gonna meet this pretty lady?"

"Tomorrow at the cook-off. Now, how about those keys?" Johnny had left his beater truck in Kerrville, so he was currently sans wheels.

Johnny carefully pulled Harrison's truck onto the highway. Acceleration in this piece of garbage was iffy. He really missed driving a vehicle that didn't belch smoke every time it backfired—something like his brand-new Jaguar.

He had to give Harrison the "drive a wreck" award of the year. This one definitely surpassed his own old pickup in decrepitude. Not only did the truck sound as if it was about to take its last gasp, the cab smelled suspiciously like wet wool. Good Lord, the man had been keeping company with a bunch of sheep! The odor of wet dog was one thing; damp sheep was an entirely different situation. Just as well that Marci's sense of humor was in good working order.

MARCI FOLLOWED Johnny out to the oldest, ugliest truck she'd ever seen. She wasn't sure she was dressed for his latest Sanford and Son vehicle.

"It's not as bad as it appears," Johnny said, although the look on his face contradicted his statement.

He turned around so quickly she almost bowled him over.

"Sorry." She was close enough that she could tell he'd showered with Irish Spring. Funny, she'd never thought soap was sexy, but it was. She needed every bit of will-power not to grab his shirt and nuzzle right into it.

"I'm not," he said as he ran his hands up and down her arms. "Sorry, I mean." Without another word, he lowered his head and took her mouth in a long, slow kiss. One touch of his lips and Marci was a goner—she forgot they were in a busy parking lot. *Again.* All her doubts and fears were lost in the wonder of his kiss.

Holy cow! That was her first reaction when she came back to her senses. Holy, holy cow!

Johnny seemed to be having the same response as he gently pushed her back and gave her a steady look. "That was, uh—" he shook his head "—that was won-derful." He pulled off his hat and combed his fingers through his hair. "Look, I'm really sorry about the truck." He peered over his shoulder at the offensive vehicle. "Maybe I can get a taxi."

"I doubt it. Don't worry, you might have to winch me up in it, but I'm game."

"That's what I love about you," Johnny said, kissing her on the nose.

Did he really say love? she wondered. And what did he mean? Was it like *I love enchiladas* or was he subtly trying to say *I love you?*

Damn it—she'd been around the block more than once and she still couldn't decipher the workings of a man's mind.

Chapter Twenty

"This is my favorite kind of place," Marci said, grinning at the 1950s-era diner with its chrome siding and neon sign.

"I used to come here with Harrison, but that was years ago. I hope the food's still as delicious as it used to be."

The smell of sizzling onions tickled her appetite. "I'm starving. The bag of Cheetos didn't last as long as I thought it would." After they'd pigged out on the iridescent orange treats, Marci had vowed not to eat for at least a week—and never to eat anything orange ever again. Except maybe an actual orange...

Johnny led her to a booth at the back of the diner. Almost before they sat down, a waitress came barreling over with a pot of coffee in her hand.

"You folks want some coffee," she drawled in the twang distinctive of West Texas.

"Please." Johnny pushed his cup toward her.

"Don't I know you?" She had filled his cup and was staring at him, the picture of concentration with one hand propped on her hip.

"Nope."

"I'm sure I do. I'll just have to think on it." The

waitress gave him a narrowed look, then ambled back to the counter, flirting with a couple of truckers on the way.

"What on earth was she talking about?"

Johnny answered with a shrug.

Please God his picture wasn't on an FBI flyer.

JOHNNY WAS ABOUT TO dig into his salad when his own worst nightmare walked into the diner—Harrison and Carlton. Or at least he assumed it was his old pal Carlton. What the hell were they doing at the diner?

Even worse, they were heading straight toward his table.

He was gonna kill 'em and tell God they died of natural causes.

"Hey, buddy," Harrison said, slapping his Stetson against his leg, creating a cloud of dust.

As Johnny frowned, Carlton Summerville mimicked the hat routine. If he'd bumped into this guy on the street he wouldn't have recognized him. He was maybe a hundred pounds heavier than the last time they'd seen each other. A hundred pounds heavier and a head of hair lighter—now, that was an interesting combination.

"Johnny, buddy, what's it been? Fifteen, twenty years?" Carlton asked as he scooted into Johnny's side of the booth. "You don't mind if we join you, do ya?"

Johnny was so flabbergasted at their nerve, he could barely remember his own name, but he did finally manage to introduce them to Marci.

"Howdy, ma'am. I'm sure pleased to meet ya," Harrison said as he sat down next to Marci.

For a guy who had a master's degree in finance, he sounded strangely like Gabby Hayes.

"We've known Johnny boy for more years than I like to count," Harrison revealed and then laughed at his own joke. "Shoot, we were friends with him when he thought gettin' three sheets to the wind would impress a girl."

"Do you remember the time he put a goat in my room? That beast pooped on my bed and ate my socks before I got back from class." Carlton provided that anecdote.

Just recalling the incident sent Harrison and Carlton into gales of laughter.

Johnny wasn't amused and Marci looked more than a bit puzzled.

"Sorry, ma'am, we got a little carried away." Harrison was the first to apologize, but Carlton quickly backed him up.

"Please call me Marci. Ma'am makes me feel like I'm your mother." Her request brought another hoot of laughter.

"Lord in heaven, you don't even vaguely resemble my mother. You're a right pretty lady. Not that my mama wasn't pretty," Carlton said quickly. Harrison merely smiled.

What was it with the two Stooges routine? Johnny was tempted to throttle them.

"Miz Marci, I have to apologize for the truck. That piece of junk could gag a maggot. We had this ewe that dropped a lamb during one of our gully washers and I hauled her to the vet in that truck. I never have been able to get the smell out."

"It's not too bad," Marci said with a smile.

"That's a *nice* lady you've got here, Johnny boy."

Harrison addressed his next comment to Marci. "So I understand you and your sister are competitors in J. W. Watson's cook-off."

Marci graced Johnny's friend with her melt-a-guy's-heart smile.

"Yes, we are. It's been quite an adventure. We're having a lot of fun."

"I'm sure J.W. would be mighty happy to hear that." Carlton punched Johnny on the arm. "Don't you think, *Johnny?*"

With friends like that, who needed enemies?

"Would you like to join us for supper?" Marci asked.

Before either man could answer, Johnny jumped in. "They were just waiting until a table opened up, isn't that right, guys?" Never mind that there were half a dozen empty ones nearby.

"Oh, sure," Carlton answered. "Miz Marci, before I amble over there to get a thick T-bone, I'd like to invite you and your sister to stay at my ranch near Alpine. It's an easy drive into Marfa for the next cook-off and our place is a damned sight more comfortable than a hotel." He turned to Johnny. "And I expect you to stay with us, too. You need to come see what I've done with my spread."

"That's incredibly nice, Mr. Summerville. I'll talk to my sister."

"Call me Carlton, and speaking of your sister, I understand from Johnny here that she's always ready to try something new."

Great, now Marci was going to know they'd been talking about her. Johnny tried to signal his friend to call a halt to the chatter, but that was like cutting off a telemarketer in the middle of a spiel.

"Tell your sis I'll teach her how to barrel race," Carlton started to prattle on, then Johnny pointed toward an empty table.

WOULDN'T THAT BE up Sissy's alley? The meal had become practically a three-ring circus, Marci thought as she dredged a French fry through the ketchup. Carlton and Harrison seemed nice enough, although she suspected they were exaggerating their accents. They sounded like they should be in an old Roy Rogers movie.

"If we decide to visit your ranch, I want you to promise me you won't tempt Sissy with riding a bucking bronc, or even worse, a bull."

"Scout's honor, pretty lady. Scout's honor."

Marci doubted they had a Scout troop out in the middle of the prairie, and that was exactly where she suspected Carlton lived. Right in the smack-dab middle of nowhere.

Carlton got up and Harrison popped up a second after his friend. "Come on down for a stay, now, ya hear?"

There was nothing like West Texas hospitality.

Chapter Twenty-One

"Don't you love the whole rodeo gig," Sissy commented as she ogled a cowboy who was leading a huge bay gelding. "I *so* appreciate a fine butt."

Marci could only shake her head. Sissy was right. A man in a pair of well-fitting jeans and cowboy boots was incredibly appealing. "That guy was young enough to be your son."

Sissy smacked her on the arm. "I might be old, but I'm not dead. At our age a fine-looking young man is like a sunset, beautiful and untouchable. And—" she paused with typical Sissy emphasis "—*your* man with the fine butt is definitely touchable."

Oh, yeah. It was time to quit messing around and get to the main attraction. And where had *that* come from?

The main attraction—good grief!

Marci and Sissy wandered down to the arena to watch the barrel racing competition. It was a sport that required nerves of steel, complete confidence in your horse and years of practice. Add a smidgen of youthful determination and a bunch of expensive equipment, and you had a prize-winning barrel racer.

"Can you believe those girls do that?" Marci asked

as a cute blonde, dressed from head to toe in hot pink, whizzed around the barrels to the whoopin' and hollerin' of her loyal audience.

"I'll bet she's been doing it since she was knee-high to a grasshopper."

"You mean like that little tyke." Marci indicated a pigtailed preschooler astride a chubby pony. Her legs stuck straight out, reminding Marci of a wobbling Weeble toy in a cowboy hat.

"We should be helping Harvey. He said the brisket would be done in about an hour, and we've been gone at least that long," Sissy said as she turned to go back to the convention center.

Marci nodded. It wasn't fair to dump everything on Harvey. Plus, they had hordes of people to feed. It seemed the entire population of West Texas had decided to attend the rodeo and cook-off. Marci couldn't figure out whether it was the food, the lure of being on the Nashville Network or a free Vince McDowell concert.

"I've been thinking about those calls you've been getting," Sissy said as she eyed another good-looking cowboy.

"I'm convinced Bill is your anonymous caller. If he really is living in Mexico, I'll bet his cell reception is terrible," Sissy said. "Although calling you a bitch doesn't sound like him. Are you *sure* that's what you heard?"

"I don't know. The voice was distorted."

"Who could it be besides Bill?"

"Beats me. I thought it was him, too, but now I don't know."

"Bill or not, if you continue to get those calls, you should tell your phone company or the cops or someone."

"And say what?" Marci asked.

Sissy stopped, hands on her hips. "That someone's threatening you."

"If you want to get technical, I wasn't threatened. Although I have to admit it was a bit scary. And if for some reason it *is* Bill, I'd rather not have the police involved."

"What does Johnny say?"

"He thinks I should have the phone company trace them. However—" she paused and shrugged eloquently "—I seriously can't see Bill being the culprit."

"Neither can I," Sissy reluctantly agreed. She twined her arm through Marci's. "Let's go kick some butt, cooking-style. And if Idabelle gets anywhere near us, I'm gonna kick *real* butt."

Marci laughed at the idea of her sister taking on Idabelle Cornell. "She's mean as a junkyard dog."

Sissy blew on her fingernails. "Honey," she drawled. "I'm planning to outwit her. She's not the brightest bulb on the Christmas tree."

"Let me know if you need help." A little altercation, especially if it didn't involve fisticuffs, might be entertaining. "Where are the kittens?" Marci asked in a quick non sequitur.

"I found a friendly janitor who let me leave them in a closet."

"It's air-conditioned, right?"

"Of course it is," Sissy snapped. "Our mama didn't raise no dummies."

"I hope Shirley doesn't climb out of the box." Fantastic. Now she was worried about "her" kitten.

"Come on, they're fine, Shirley's fine, but I'm not so sure about Harvey. He's been a bear lately."

It didn't take a rocket scientist to realize why he was

grumpy. He was considering cold-cocking Vince McDowell. Unfortunately, or fortunately, as the case might be, the skinny little singing cowboy didn't have a clue he was about to have a run-in with the terminator, disguised as a mild-mannered CPA.

"Okay, I—" Before Marci could finish, her cell phone rang. This time a garbled voice told her she was being watched. Good Lord, it *was* a stalker!

"What was that?"

"Um, I don't know. Someone said they're watching me."

Sissy's squeal was ear-splitting. "We're definitely calling the cops! Was it a man or a woman?"

"I couldn't tell—the voice was distorted. And forget it. We're not calling the cops. We'd sound like a couple of bimbos. First of all, *why* would someone watch me? And second, I always have people around me, so what harm could they do?"

"You should tell Johnny," Sissy said urgently. "He'll take care of it."

Maybe she'd tell him—and maybe she wouldn't. She hadn't relied on a man in quite a while and wasn't ready to slip back into that role.

"I'll think about it," Marci said to assuage Sissy's impending hysteria. "We need to get back to cookin'." She grabbed her sister's hand and steered her over to the line of barbecue pits.

The Ozona cook-off presented a different environment from the previous ones. The booths were inside the building and the actual cooking was done outside. Poor Harvey, there was an awning that provided shade, but the temperature was just a little above hellish.

"There, baby," Sissy cooed as she took a handkerchief out of his back pocket and wiped his face. "You're such a trouper."

Marci suspected he'd rather be called sexy, dashing or at the very least, handsome. And he *was* all of the above, in his own Harvey fashion.

The sisters basted the ribs and brisket. And for this venue they'd added chicken. Hell. This had to be hell, Marci thought as she felt a trickle of sweat make its way down her cleavage to her waistband. Then she spotted someone who was as out of place as a pig at a tea party.

"Look at that guy," Marci whispered to her sister. "Don't look," she snapped when Sissy started to turn around.

"You said 'look.' I was gonna look, you dumb bunny."

"I meant take a peek. He's over by the beer vendor."

"Please, half the guys at this thing are regular patrons of the beer vendor." Sissy raised an eyebrow. "Is he good-looking?"

"You. Are. Incorrigible." Marci barely resisted the urge to knock her sister upside the head. "He's ugly and he's covered in tattoos. If he's not a gangbanger, I'll eat my hat." Marci peered over at him again, and to her horror he was staring at *her*.

"Yeew! He looks like he just stepped out of a grade-B Pancho Villa movie. I'm absolutely positive he's packin' heat."

"Packin' heat?" Sissy exclaimed. "Packin' heat!" She broke into gales of laughter.

Without another word, Marci marched back into the tent in search of something cold to drink. Instead she found her handsome cowboy.

"What time are you finished tonight?" Johnny asked.

He ran a finger down her cheek. "Why don't you stay inside where it's cool? You look flushed."

"The judges are supposed to show up at five o'clock. The minute they leave I'm outta here," Marci said. "I'd kill for a cold drink."

Johnny gave her a light kiss. "Come with me. You want a Coke or something stronger?"

"A Coke," she said as she followed Johnny into the conference center. "Sissy is part of the reason I'm flushed." She explained about the Pancho Villa wannabe. For some reason, she decided to omit the "gonna watch you" part of her phone call.

"He was staring at you?" Johnny asked.

"Well, I thought he was. Maybe he wasn't. Why would he want to stare at a couple of senior citizens?"

"Sexy seniors."

"Okay, sexy seniors. Or at least Sissy is."

Johnny raised her face for another kiss. "You are *very* sexy, and desirable and lovely."

That was nice to hear. And the feeling was mutual. She might as well admit it to herself: she was in love.

"How about dinner?"

"Don't you have to stay for Vince's concert?"

"Vince can handle it himself."

That was a weird comment for an employee to make.

AFTER MARCI HAD AGREED to dinner and he'd escorted her safely back to Sissy and Harv, Johnny went in search of Pancho. The phone calls had bothered him. Now the threat was elevated. Anyone who wanted to hurt his lady would have to go through him.

Johnny looked high and low—the rodeo arena, the men's room, the horse trailers—and shoot, he even asked someone to check out the ladies' dressing room. Pancho was gone. There wasn't anyone who even vaguely resembled Marci's description.

She might have imagined him. Nope, not a possibility. The idea that the guy might really be a stalker made Johnny's skin crawl.

The next stop was Vince's trailer. It was time to bring in the professionals—his pal's bodyguard.

"Hey, my friend, come on in," Vince said. "Would you like a beer?"

"Sure." Johnny made himself at home in the seating area. "I need a favor."

"Anything." Vince handed him a longneck as he plopped down in an overstuffed chair.

"I'd like to borrow Brunhilda for a couple of days." That was the nickname Vince's female bodyguard had earned when she took out a two-hundred-pound overzealous fan. Fortunately, she loved the moniker.

"She's yours. Now I'm dying to know why you need her."

Johnny was hesitant to fill him in on all the details but finally decided to provide his friend with the basics.

"Brunhilda's gonna love it," Vince said as he reached for his cell phone. "Let's get her over here so you can give her the facts.

BARBECUE, BARBECUE, BARBECUE—Marci was sick of barbecue. She plastered a smile on her face and continued to pile small samples of brisket on paper plates.

"That's a great shot, Miz Hamilton," the cameraman said as he panned both the crowd and the action in the booth.

"Miz Aguirre, tell me all about your win at Luckenbach."

Good. He could bother Sissy, who reveled in the attention.

"Would you like some of our barbecue?" Marci handed a plate to a wiry little man wearing the oldest cowboy hat she'd ever laid eyes on.

"Thank ya very much, ma'am," he said as he tipped his hat.

Ma'am, ma'am! The man was at least eighty and he was calling her ma'am. Talk about making her feel ancient.

She was still pondering the age issue when she looked up into a face that only his mother could love. Pancho!

"Don't worry. I'm here to watch you."

What, what, *what?* "Sissy, Sissy!" Marci screeched.

"He's here, he's here." When Marci whirled back around, the man had disappeared into the crowd.

"Who was here?"

"The guy I was telling you about! The one I saw outside. Pancho."

"Pancho?" Sissy looked like she was about to vault the table to go search for the offender.

"He's gone, vanished, disappeared."

"Damn. Did he say anything?"

Marci was hesitant to reveal what he'd said because Sissy was going to flip out. "He told me not to worry— that he's here to watch me."

"Oh, my God!"

"Uh, huh."

"You tell Johnny now, you hear?"

Yep, she heard. She just wasn't sure she'd do it.

THE REST OF THE DAY was uneventful, except for the cook-off results. The good news was that they came in second; the bad news was they were now tied with Idabelle for first place points. That was enough to make a girl nervous. The woman was certainly sleazy, but was she capable of sabotaging their cooking? If that wasn't her motive, why was she always lurking around?

"I'm going out back to help Harvey clean the barbecue pit," Sissy said as she took off her apron.

"I'm right behind you." Marci said. "But first I'm gonna check on Shirley." She headed over to the janitor's closet in the air conditioned convention center where the cats were sequestered.

Mama Cat and the kittens were fine, although Shirley was in a mop bucket. For a nanosecond, Marci reconsidered her choice of kittens—then decided no way, Shirley was a carbon copy of Sissy. Feisty, mischievous and full of adventure.

Marci put Shirley in the box with her siblings, hoping a good dinner would entice her to stay put, at least for a few minutes. The little scamps were incredibly funny, and when they all finally asserted their independence Sissy was going to have her hands full. Served her right. She'd better start looking for some good homes.

Marci was returning to their booth when she stopped in her tracks. Wait a minute. Someone was skulking around, and that someone was Idabelle Cornell. Damn it! She was messing with the sauce they'd left on the stove.

Can you say e-coli?

Should she run outside to get Sissy and risk her creating mayhem, or round up a security guard? That was a no-brainer, but where was a rent-a-cop when she needed one? Did they even *have* security guys in

Ozona? She should probably talk to a deputy sheriff, but what exactly would she tell him? That she'd caught one of the other competitors tasting their sauce?

How lame was that?

When in doubt, go with benign confrontation. "Hey, what do you think you're doing?" she called.

Idabelle momentarily looked nonplussed, and then quickly regained her chutzpah. "I thought you left the fire on. I was just tryin' to help."

"Yeah, sure."

"Have it your way." Idabelle fluffed her hair. "Don't look at me if something goes wrong with your cooking." She pranced out of the booth as if she owned the world.

That sounded like a threat. What had happened to good old-fashioned competition? It had obviously gone down the drain. Marci was about to find Sissy when out of the corner of her eye she saw Idabelle deep in conversation with a woman wearing a cowboy hat and a huge pair of sunglasses.

Call it intuition or call it being nosy—Marci decided to eavesdrop. She crept around the adjacent booth and hid behind a banner.

Darn it! She was too far away to hear what they were saying. However, she did notice that Idabelle glanced at their booth several times during the course of her talk with the unidentified woman. Then, when Idabelle shook her head as if she was confirming something and the woman opened her purse and handed over a wad of bills, the hair on the back of Marci's neck stood straight up.

That didn't look good, but why would some stranger be bribing Idabelle—especially to harm them?

It was time to track down Harvey, Marci decided as she headed out the exit. Telling Miss Ditz was out of the question.

It was almost evening and Vince's concert was in full swing, so the area outside the tent was deserted and dark. If Marci had been the least bit skittish, she'd have high tailed it back inside, where the lights were bright and a few people still lingered. Idabelle and the mystery woman, for instance. Marci was almost inside when that thought entered her head. *Scaredy cat,* she told herself. It was just a dark parking lot.

Just a dark parking lot, just a dark parking lot—it seemed like a great mantra until she ran smack dab into...Pancho. The bad-ass who looked like he should be sporting a bandolier.

He grabbed her arm, and Marci screamed loudly enough to wake the dead.

"Señora, por favor."

Marci screeched even louder. She hadn't been hysterical since she was sixteen and had crashed into a cop car, but this time she was tuning up for a huge hissy.

"Señora!"

Marci took a breath in preparation for—what? Shrieking, screaming or running like hell? Before her brain had a chance to send a message to her feet, salvation arrived in the form of a tiny redheaded dervish who took Pancho down like a tenpin in a strike. *That* was a black belt move.

Pancho scrambled to his feet and ran before Marci's newest heroine could trip him.

"Darn it! He got away," the petite Ninja groused as she pulled herself up to her full five-foot-one-inch frame and dusted off the seat of her skin-tight Wranglers.

"Uh, um, who are you?"

"I'm Vicky Valsora. I'm one of Vince's bodyguards." She stuck out her hand. "I'm supposed to be keeping an eye on you."

"On *me*?"

"Yeah, Johnny said you might need some help. I guess he was right."

"You're guarding me?"

"I sure am. And I'm good at my job, although that guy got the drop on me…*this* time." A look of consternation crossed her face. "I can guarantee he won't be that lucky again. They don't call me Brunhilda for nothin'."

Marci wanted to sputter, to jump up and down, and most of all she wanted to punch Mr. Johnny Walker. How dare he presume to hire someone to guard her?

And how incredibly sweet was that? The big jerk really cared about her.

Before Marci could stop Vicky—or Brunhilda or whatever her name was—she was on the phone to Johnny.

"He attacked her."

Vicky held the phone away from her ear, allowing Marci to get an earful. She didn't realize Johnny knew that many colorful words.

"She's fine. You want to talk to her?" Vicky looked relieved as she practically threw the phone at Marci.

"Hi." That was about as innocuous as she could get.

"Don't move, I'll be there in less than a minute," he commanded and hung up before she could reply.

JOHNNY SNAPPED his phone shut and ran across the parking lot like a wild man. When he heard the word *attacked* he almost had a seizure. Someone had threatened the woman he loved. By God, he planned to spend the rest of his life with that lady, and heaven help the idiot who messed with her.

It took a mere three minutes to sprint across a field and a parking lot. Not bad for an old boy, huh?

"Are you okay?" He skidded to a stop where the two ladies were sitting on a curb, talking like old friends.

"I'm fine. Vicky did all the work." Marci smiled at Vince's bodyguard.

"God!" Johnny had to sit down before his knees gave way. "That scared me to death."

"Join the crowd," Marci said.

"Thanks, Vic. I owe you," Johnny panted. "This lady isn't going to leave my sight until we figure out what's happening. We may need you later."

"Sure, Johnny. Glad to help. You have my number— give me a call," Vicky said, then she strolled off.

"Wow. She's so little and—"

"Spunky," Johnny tossed in.

"Yeah, *spunky* works."

"She's a martial arts expert. Before she went to work for Vince she was a stuntwoman."

"Those redheads are dangerous." Marci laughed, thinking of her sister. Although Sissy's hair color came from a bottle, the temperament came straight from her soul.

AFTER JOHNNY AND Marci had retrieved the cats from the closet, they went in search of Harvey and Sissy. Their dinner date was forgotten in all the excitement.

"You and Sissy should take Carlton up on his invitation. His ranch is the safest place I know of. He has over two dozen cowhands and they all know their way around a Remington."

That sounded great. She did *not* want a repeat visit from Pancho.

"And Carlton will teach Sissy how to barrel race."

"I like to go fast, but I want to do it in a Porsche, not on a horse. I'd love a sports car, wouldn't you?"

Johnny was spared answering when Marci noticed her sister. After lots of squealing and "I'll kill that sorry sucker," the sisters disengaged themselves and got down to business.

After all was said and done, and with a lot of input from Johnny, they decided to spend the week at Carlton's ranch.

Good choice.

Chapter Twenty-Two

"It's beautiful here," Marci exclaimed as they drove up to a sprawling white ranch house nestled among cool green trees.

Folks tended to think that Texas was just a huge throwback to the Ponderosa. Boy, were they wrong—except about the size.

North to south, east to west, Texas was gigantic. Just ask anyone who'd ever driven it, mile after mile—after mile.

Texas was wild.

Texas was beautiful.

Best of all, Texas had something for every taste. If you wanted sophisticated city life, you loved Dallas and Houston.

If fun and fiestas turned you on, San Antonio was your city.

If you were looking for oom pah bands and sauerkraut, you wouldn't want to bypass Fredericksburg.

Academia and politics? Austin was ideal.

However, if the wild beauty of the high desert plains and the stark magnificence of the Davis Mountains appealed to you, Alpine would be your idea of heaven.

And Carlton's 300,000-acre spread was in the middle of those mountains and that desert. It was the optimal place to meditate, watch the wildlife, play cowboy, and best of all hide out from an ersatz Pancho Villa.

"I haven't been here in years. Carlton's done a good job," Johnny said.

Marci wasn't sure how she'd been talked into visiting the Summerville ranch, but now that she was here she planned to enjoy everything about the experience. Okay, maybe not *everything*. She was definitely skipping the steer wrestling, the buckin' broncs and the mountain oysters.

When they reached the house, Marci noticed Carlton and two gorgeous women standing on the porch. They were grinning like they'd won the lottery. Then her attention was on Johnny, who'd jumped out of the convertible and sprinted up the steps before Marci could get her seat belt off.

Why did he have the Naomi Judd look-alike enveloped in a bear hug? Marci seriously thought about burning rubber. But she was not, repeat not jealous!

Uh, huh, and pigs were hang gliding off those nearby hills.

Darn—what if she was an old girlfriend, or even worse, his ex-wife? No, no, no. Marci was *not* going to borrow trouble. Not. Not. Not.

So in for a penny, etc. Marci did the logical thing and let her sister take over. Sissy had always bragged about being the oldest, so she could be in charge.

"What's with the brunette?" Sissy asked as she retrieved the carton of cats from the back of the Suburban.

Marci shrugged. "I can't look. Please tell me they're not exchanging spit."

Sissy peeked around the end of the SUV. "Nope, no kissing. Wait, he just did it."

"I'm gonna kill him," Marci said, then sucked in a deep breath. "Nope. I'm a lady. I don't have any claim on him. He can kiss anyone he wants."

"Really?" Sissy used her most dubious voice.

"Really. I'll just pretend he isn't here. Mr. Walker is about to meet the Grand Duchess of the Ice Kingdom."

"Oh, boy," Harvey muttered as he carried the box of kittens. He had apparently heard Marci and Sissy's discussion. "That old boy's in a mess of trouble."

"Ain't that the truth," Sissy agreed before she marched up the steps, a kitten in each hand.

"Hi, Carlton. Thanks for inviting us. I brought you a little gift. Don't worry. By the time we leave, these babies will be weaned." She handed him the two kittens.

Only Sissy could get away with giving kittens as a hostess gift.

"Hi." She turned to the women. "I'm Sissy Aguirre, and that's my sister, Marci Hamilton, lurking down by the car."

Marci heard that. *Lurking!* She lifted her chin, upped the chill factor and marched up the stairs as if she'd just been invited to tea with the queen.

About the time Marci made it to the top step, Johnny seemed to snap out of his trance. Perhaps it was the icy demeanor or maybe it was the electrical sparks she was emitting, but he stepped away from the brunette like she had a communicable disease.

"Marci," he said with forced joviality. J. W. Watson recognized a pissed-off puppy when he saw one. "Let me introduce some old friends. Stacy—" he indicated the woman standing next to his buddy "—is Carlton's wife. And this is Charlene." Johnny took the other woman's hand and pulled her forward. "She's one of my oldest friends."

Somehow, not being a dummy and all, Johnny didn't think it was a good idea to introduce Charlene as his high school sweetheart.

Marci soldiered on through the introductions, even though Johnny suspected her molars were about to crack. She was jealous. Hot damn, the woman was jealous!

"I should probably get on home. It's my turn to take the twins to softball practice," Charlene said.

"Oh, you have twins. I have twin granddaughters," Marci said.

What a lady. She was cordial even when she was big-time irritated.

"The twins are my grandkids, too. I have seven grown children." Charlene laughed as she poked Johnny. "Can you believe my big lug of a husband is an expert at French braiding? With seven daughters, it became a matter of self-preservation." She checked her watch. "Gotta run. Stacy, I'll call ya. And it was real nice meeting you ladies." With that farewell, Charlene was down the steps and into her pickup.

Marci was jealous, and that meant she cared. He could work with that.

"Let me show you the guest house. It has three bedrooms and a swimming pool. Johnny, I thought you might want to stay up here at the main house," Stacy said.

Well, damn.

Carlton grabbed one of the duffel bags and steered their guests in the direction of the outlying buildings.

"Y'all get unpacked and come on back up to the house, ya hear? We're gonna have a barbecue," he said.

Marci's spirits dropped like a rock. No, not barbecue again!

THE JOHNNY/CHARLENE experience was disconcerting.
Marci would bet her retirement that although Charlene
might be married and have a gazillion kids, she and
Johnny had once been an item. Did it matter? Maybe it
did, maybe it didn't. And why was she so upset about
it, anyway?

Because she was in love with the guy, and what was
she going to do about *that*?

"OUR MR. WALKER'S a smart guy," Sissy murmured as
she unpacked her bag.

Marci didn't miss the fact that her sister had claimed
the bedroom with a door adjoining Harvey's. She wasn't
about to comment on her sister's maneuver.

"What do you mean?" Marci asked. Her bedroom
was on the other side of the house and that might also
prove convenient.

"I mean he got the drift that you're peeved and he's
making himself scarce."

Marci laughed at her sister's accurate assessment. She
had quickly recovered from her snit; however, he didn't
need to know that. There was something incredibly appealing about a guy who was willing to grovel.

"I say we go find Mr. Johnny and yank his chain,"
Marci said with a twinkle in her eye.

"Sounds like a plan to me." Sissy twined her arm
through Marci's. "Chest out. Wonderbra in place."

"Check."

"Chin up."

"Check."

"Smile on."

"Yep, plus lots of lip gloss."

"Big hair."

Marci glanced at Sissy's spiky red do and laughed.

"Not anytime soon."

"I say let's find Mr. Johnny and turn his world upside down," Sissy suggested.

Why not? He'd already sent Marci's world skittering off its axis.

"ARE YOU READY to do some barrel racing?" Carlton asked after he and Sissy had enjoyed more than a couple of cold Lone Stars that evening.

"Absolutely," Sissy declared. Harvey simply shook his head.

"Um, sister." Marci hated to be a party-pooper, but the dimwit could fall off and break a bone. "You haven't been on a horse in twenty years. Do you really think riding is a good idea? We're not talking about jogging along on a pony."

Sissy put her arm around Marci's shoulders. "We only live once and I wanna do this," she said with a giggle and a hiccup.

"Merciful heavens," Marci muttered. She exchanged an exasperated glance with Harvey.

"Let's sit in the swing," Johnny whispered. Before she knew what had happened, they were nestled in a wooden swing hanging from a low branch of a large pecan tree.

"Are you still mad at me?" He nuzzled her neck. How could she stay mad when he did that?

"Well, are you?" He'd replaced nuzzling with kisses from behind her ear all the way to the dip in her collarbone and back again.

"You're probably miffed about Charlene. I'm sorry, I forgot my manners." He had progressed to a series of little nibble kisses.

Who was Charlene?

"Seriously, I'm sorry," he mumbled between kisses. "I've known her—"

"Shut up," she demanded. "And kiss me."

"Yes, ma'am. I can do that, I surely can." And he did, and did, and did some more.

Chapter Twenty-Three

"Eeyyhh," Marci squealed as Sissy took her third splat of the day. Swear to God if she broke something Marci would never forgive her. Sometimes that silly woman forgot she wasn't a teenager.

And did the dingbat *really* think she'd be able to coax that horse around those barrels when she couldn't even stay in the saddle?

Marci was more than happy sitting in the bleachers sipping a mint julep. Thank heavens their hostess was a good southern girl who practiced hospitality.

"Why aren't you out there?"

That was a voice she loved.

"Because I'm too smart."

He sat down and brushed her lips with a brief but potent kiss.

She was in over her head. Put those big brown eyes and that smooth-as-molasses drawl together with his faded denim and scuffed boots, and you had an irresistible combination. Yup, there was something about a cowboy...

"How about I teach you to rope?"

How about they do a little more necking?

"See that cow over there?" He pointed out a red calf with a white face.

"Yes," she answered, wondering what he was getting at.

"By the end of the day you'll be able to rope him."

"I am *not* roping a baby animal. End of sentence."

Her proclamation sent him into gales of laughter. "Okay, I'll teach you how to rope a fence post. When you get proficient at that, you can practice on Carlton's wheelbarrow."

"You're kidding, right?"

"Nope. Come with me." He picked up her Stetson and placed it on her head. "Now that you *look* like a cowgirl, you want to act like one?"

DURING THE NEXT couple of days, Sissy spent most of her time in the Jacuzzi working out the kinks, and Marci became obsessed with trying to rope the darned wheelbarrow that had a wooden cow head attached to the front.

Schmaltzy—the whole exercise was the ultimate in schmaltzy.

"Once more and then I'm finished, done, not going to do this anymore," Sissy declared as she wheeled the ersatz cow around the arena.

"Aw, come on. I haven't said a word about watching you fly off the horse." Marci raised the lasso to try again but was stopped in mid-throw by that mesmerizing drawl she craved.

"Why don't I take you ladies to lunch."

Sunglasses, Stetson, faded jeans—how could a girl resist an invitation from a man wearing that?

"Absolutely. I'm hungry enough to eat a horse.

Oops, I shouldn't say that on a ranch," Sissy said as she ditched the bovine garden equipment. "Where are we going?"

JOHNNY LOOPED AN ARM around Marci's shoulders. The past two days could be counted among the best in his life. He had vowed not to press Marci into anything that might make her uncomfortable. But it was obvious, at least to him, that it was time to ramp up their relationship.

"I thought we'd go to the Lone Star Café in Alpine. Carlton says their burgers are the size of dinner plates and the iced tea comes in half-gallon Mason jars."

"My idea of heaven," Sissy said.

"Let's do it," Marci agreed, and they piled into one of the Bar S ranch trucks.

There were a few things Johnny was looking forward to in the near future: driving his own car, getting Marci alone someplace with a nice soft bed and telling her the truth. After all this time—and duplicity—that last one might be a problem. Pray God, it wouldn't be insurmountable.

"Carlton was right. The food is delicious," Marci said half an hour later as she dug into a piece of coconut cream pie.

"Uh, huh," Sissy murmured without having to say a word.

"Have you had any more of those calls?" Johnny asked. Although he assumed she would've told him, they'd been busy. Courting took a lot of effort.

Marci looked uncomfortable. "I've kept my phone off and deleted any messages that were suspicious."

"Have you had any?" Johnny asked.

"What?"

"Suspicious messages."

Marci shrugged as she scraped up the last bit of whipped cream. "Some."

"How many is some? One or a hundred?" Johnny wanted to rant and rave. Knowing that wouldn't go over well, he took a deep breath instead.

"About five, give or take a couple."

Five! That did it! He'd either have to cajole Vince into lending him Brunhilda, aka Vicky Valsora, again, or he could have Brian hire the best P.I. in Texas. Whatever was happening here, it had to come to a screeching halt.

THE RIDE BACK to the ranch was tense. Even Sissy couldn't get a conversation going, and she could talk to a wall. Marci knew she shouldn't have told Johnny about the calls, but lying was foreign to her character.

"I'd like to talk to you about something," Johnny said when they arrived at the ranch.

"Okay." Marci followed him to the swing. Of all the beautiful places on the ranch, that was her favorite. The shade of the pecan tree provided welcome relief from the blistering heat of the sun.

"I'd like you to spend a couple of days with me at the Palacio Hotel in Marfa."

"Uh…" Marci started to say that sounded great, but Johnny didn't let her get a word in edgewise. Her sexy cowboy was babbling like a pimply-faced adolescent with his first crush.

Did she ever love that man!

Chapter Twenty-Four

The fourth and final cook-off was scheduled for the Festival of Lights in Marfa. Located deep in the heart of Big Bend country, Marfa was probably best known for the spectral Marfa Lights that had danced and played across the desert for hundreds, maybe even thousands, of years.

Although scientists had tried to discover the origin of the ethereal phenomenon, the ghost lights were still as much a mystery in the twenty-first century as they'd been in the 1800s. The locals had adopted a "let 'em be" policy, but that didn't keep people from congregating at the designated viewing area to enjoy the show.

Alien spacecraft, swamp gas, astral projections, atmospheric phenomenon—who knew? And who cared as long as the good folks of Marfa could watch their reddish orange illuminations as they cavorted across the desert floor.

"This hotel is fantastic." The Palacio was a throwback to a time when interstate highways were nonexistent, movies were epic and the Model T was king.

"Look at this." She was enraptured by a display of James Dean memorabilia, a tribute to the classic western movie, *Giant,* that was filmed in Marfa. For Marci everything about the Palacio was love at first sight.

And speaking of love… Marci was enthralled, enchanted and entranced by Johnny Walker, the man she now freely admitted she loved.

She was scared out of her mind.

Her relationship with Bill had barely progressed to any real intimacy. And he was in his seventies. Johnny, on the other hand, was much younger and obviously in good shape.

Sharing a bed meant taking off her clothes, and taking off her clothes sent up all kinds of red flags. Her body reminded her of an old house; it had settled it some unusual places.

"You're thinking too much." Johnny opened the ornately carved door and escorted her into a fabulous art deco room. "If you're uncomfortable with this, let me know." He cupped her chin and lowered his mouth to give her a lingering kiss. A kiss that made her feel young and sexy and horny as all heck.

"We can go back to the ranch if you prefer."

"Like hell," she answered. "Come here, big boy."

His kiss had awakened a riot of feelings she thought were dormant. Was the euphoria of love and lust and a whole host of emotions she couldn't name enough to stifle that little voice screaming "cellulite, cellulite, cellulite?"

"You're thinking again." This time he had one hand entwined in her hair while his fingers explored the buttons running down the front of her blouse.

"You're beautiful, absolutely beautiful." That lazy, sexy baritone of his was better than an aphrodisiac.

"Uh, huh." Conversation was highly overrated.

Pop went the first button as he bent his head to kiss every inch of skin he'd uncovered.

When the second button slid through its hole, he lowered his head and alternated between her neck and her cleavage.

The third button revealed her lavender lace bra. Her first thought was praise God for Victoria's Secret; her second, very peripheral thought, was that her Penney's cotton undies were history.

"You have too many clothes on," Marci observed before she ripped open the snaps on his western shirt revealing a *really* fine body.

"Oh, yeah," she murmured as she backed toward the bed. "Oh definitely, yes." That was her last cogent thought before the backs of her legs nudged up against the edge of that beautiful bed.

"UMM…THAT WAS…" What did you say about something that was perfect? Marci's head was resting on his chest while she played with the crinkly curls.

She could feel the rumble of his laugh.

"That was what?"

She responded with a chuckle of her own. "That was yummy."

"And speaking of yummy…" He punctuated his words with a delicious kiss. Being with Johnny was like coming home. It felt as if they'd been lovers for years—a mesmerizing combination of old and new, comfortable and erotic.

Youthful enthusiasm had nothing on a man who was seasoned. Just ask the Pointer Sisters; they had the right idea about a man with a slow hand and an easy touch. And Marci's favorite cowboy was a man with a *very* slow hand.

"I'm starving," Johnny said as he ran his fingers

through her hair. "Can I interest you in taking a shower?" He waggled an eyebrow suggestively. "And then we can head down to dinner. How about a big steak and a baked potato with the works?"

Marci's stomach growled in agreement. "I suppose that answers your question." At this point she was so comfortable with him, nothing could embarrass her.

"THIS REALLY IS an interesting place." Marci was commenting on the hotel lobby decorated in Mexican colonial antiques. It was appropriate to the area's blend of Texan and Mexican cultures.

"It sure is," Johnny agreed although the woman on his arm was far more beautiful.

Should he or shouldn't he kiss her neck? It was a public place and he was pushing his luck—but why not. He leaned down and nuzzled the soft skin behind her ear.

She nudged him. "Over there!"

Johnny turned around to see what she was talking about.

"Don't look," she muttered.

Johnny frowned. "What am I not supposed to look at?"

"Pancho was over there behind the potted palm."

"Pancho?" Johnny's gut tensed in anticipation. Brian had contacted the investigator, although as far as Johnny knew the guy hadn't arrived yet. "Are you telling me the man from Ozona is here?"

"Uh, huh." It was obvious that Marci was trying not to spook her stalker.

Johnny didn't share her hesitancy. "Wait here," he demanded, then marched across the lobby. If he caught the guy, he was going to beat him to a pulp—the hell with bad publicity.

"Stop right there," Johnny ordered as the mustachioed man slipped out the side door. "You're not getting away this time!" he yelled. But the man did exactly that; he vanished like a ghost.

"Crap!"

"It doesn't matter." Marci joined him on the deserted sidewalk, looking up and down the street. There wasn't a soul in sight.

"Maybe that wasn't him."

"Yeah," Johnny agreed although they both knew it almost certainly was. "Let's go eat." As soon as he could get a few private minutes, he was calling Brian. It was time to up the ante on investigators, bodyguards, or whatever the heck people used for protection. If they had to call in the cavalry, he was willing to spring for that, too. He was ready to do *anything* to keep Marci safe.

Johnny was leading her back through the lobby to the adjoining steak house when he glimpsed a petite brunette entering the elevator.

That couldn't possibly be Marina. Could it? He had to be hallucinating. Because if he wasn't, he was in a whole lot of trouble.

Johnny suddenly had the sinking feeling that Randy had accidentally mentioned Marci to his mom. And if Brian was right about Marina's obsession, he could well imagine his ex following him to West Texas.

Damn!

Chapter Twenty-Five

Marci spent a delightful two days feeling young and in love. It was like a honeymoon, only better. It took just one of Johnny's kisses to push Pancho right out of her mind.

Now, it was time to get back to reality, and reality was the cook-off and the Marfa Festival of Lights. Tomorrow the festivities began; tonight was the parade. Marci loved hometown parades and this one fit the bill perfectly.

Sissy and Harvey had secured prime spots across from the courthouse. "Did you have a good time?" Sissy's grin turned to a knowing smirk.

"I certainly did."

Sissy poked her in the ribs. "Shirley missed you."

"Uh, huh." Marci felt the heat rising up her neck. Thank goodness it was dark.

"Did you sleep well?"

That did it! "None of your business," she snapped. Hopefully that would shut Sissy up for a few minutes.

Johnny chuckled as he wrapped an arm around her shoulders. "*Did* you get any sleep?" he whispered and she wanted to melt in a puddle right there on the sidewalk.

Marci's impulse to kiss him was short-circuited by the start of the parade. It was Americana at its finest—

the high school marching band, complete with a bevy of teenage twirlers and cheerleaders, followed by the sheriff's posse, on horseback of course, plus fire, police and EMT vehicles from the three surrounding counties, and last but not least, Miss Marfa was riding in a vintage Mustang convertible.

"That was fun," Sissy said when the final equestrian team had passed by. "Do you want to go with me to check out the tent?" she asked Marci. "I'd like to see the facilities before tomorrow."

"Sure, let's go."

After a win in Luckenbach, a second place at the Ozona Rodeo, and a third place showing in Gruene, the sisters were focused on winning this leg of the competition. A triumph in Marfa would guarantee the jackpot. Marci already had the color of her VW convertible picked out.

Arm in arm they walked across the street to the courthouse square, careful to avoid the piles of horse droppings.

"Do you think they'll have this stuff picked up by tomorrow?" Sissy asked, drawing a chuckle from Johnny.

"They will, even if the mayor has to get out here and do it himself," he assured them.

The cook-off tent was located on the courthouse square. According to their bellhop, who looked like he was in middle school, everyone who was anyone would show up. Mention the words *TV camera* and people were programmed to come out of the woodwork. And if past history held, there'd be more people sporting rodeo buckles than you could shake a stick at.

It was such a kick.

JOHNNY WAS FOLLOWING the sisters when he noticed the new Escalade and Marina standing next to it. She was dressed more appropriately for lunching at the country club than a down-home parade. What really struck him was the malevolent glare she was sending him. Was she going to haunt him for the rest of his life?

That answered one question; he *had* seen Marina at the hotel. Damn, sometimes he hated to be right. Johnny briefly considered veering over to have a chat with his ex-wife, but on second thought decided that wouldn't help matters. Whatever she was up to would be bad news. Pray God it wouldn't be the death of what he had going with Marci.

Tonight he had to come clean, because if he didn't, he was a goner. And that was as sure a fact as God made little green apples.

"I'll stay out here and make a few calls," he said as they approached the entrance to the tent. "Don't leave without me, okay?" Johnny brushed his fingers against her cheek.

"Okay." She gave him a smile before she stretched up on tiptoe to kiss him.

The touch of her lips was so electric, Johnny couldn't resist deepening the kiss. The knot in his gut told him calamity was lurking around the corner.

He couldn't lose this woman, dammit! He put every bit of love he had into that kiss in an attempt to bind her to him through thick and thin. All he could do was trust that it would work.

"Wow," she murmured after he reluctantly stepped back and put his forehead on hers.

"I'm going into the tent," she said. "Other than that, I'm not going anywhere."

"I know." He shot her a grin and hoped she was right.

When she disappeared, he pulled out his phone and punched in Brian's number.

"Hey, guy. I have a huge problem," he said when his friend answered.

"Um, we have a situation here, too. I was about to call you."

Before Brian could continue, Johnny broke in. His heart was beating a mile a minute. "What's going on?"

"Randy had a wreck. He called me from the hospital and said he's okay. He sounded pretty shook up, though. That's all I know. I'm on my way to check on him now. I was going to call you after I figured out exactly what's happening."

"I'm coming home."

"I figured you would, so I made arrangements with a private pilot in Alpine to fly you home. They're waiting for you at the airport."

Johnny raked a hand through his hair. "I'll be there as soon as I can."

Everything except the thought of his son flew out of his mind as he raced to his truck.

"ARE YOU *sure* you haven't seen Johnny?" Marci asked Sissy for the fifth time. She'd also queried everyone she could find, up to and including the guys setting up the Porta-Potties, and she still didn't have a clue where he'd gone. It was like he'd been abducted by aliens.

She clutched Sissy's arm. "I think something's happened to him."

"If he's around, Harv will find him. He probably just went to eat and Carlton's truck broke down. Let's sit here and wait." Sissy pulled out two metal folding chairs and pushed her sister into one of them. "See, there's Harv." And sure enough, Harvey was making a beeline for them.

"I found someone who saw him," he said as he sat

down in another chair. "One of the guys from Vince's band said Johnny hauled out of here like there was a fire under his tail. The last time he saw him, he'd turned onto the highway going out of town."

It took every bit of Marci's willpower to keep her mouth from falling open. *He left town?* Why did he leave town?

In usual Sissy fashion, her sister took charge of the situation. "We've got a suite. You can have one of the bedrooms and Harv can sleep on the couch. Or not." Marci noted the coy look Sissy shot her ex. "Plus, Shirley and the other kittens have missed you. So are you game?"

"Okay, I guess. But what if he comes back and wonders where I am?"

"We'll leave a note at your hotel."

"Okay." Marci wasn't in the mood for a solitary night at the Palacio—especially since she was worried sick about Johnny.

She followed Sissy and Harvey to the Suburban. "Where are you staying?" she asked, even though she wasn't really interested.

"They put us up in a motel that was renovated to entice the Hollywood types." In the preceding decade, Marfa had become a sort of Wild West Left Bank for artists and art galleries.

"Is it nice?" Again, she didn't care, but felt obliged to keep up her end of the conversation.

"Very nice in a retro way."

Marci checked her cell phone. Yep, it was on and nope, no messages. Darn him, she thought as she turned off her phone. Let *him* worry when he couldn't figure out where she was.

The drawback to that was it would only work if he loved her.

Chapter Twenty-Six

The day of the cook-off dawned bright, sunny and hot. Bright and sunny was good, hot was iffy, and a missing boyfriend was the pits.

"Put on your best duds and plaster a smile on your face. We're going to win you a car," Sissy instructed as she hogged the mirror. She'd been doing that since they were in junior high and Marci was sick of it. So she did the sisterly thing and nudged her with a hip.

"My turn. You can look over the top of my head."

"Someone's in a snit this morning."

"If you want to die soon, keep it up."

Sissy put her arm around Marci's shoulders. "I'm sorry. I'm sure he wouldn't have left unless it was an emergency."

Marci nodded glumly.

Sissy picked up the kitten that was twining around her legs. "This is Barney. Give him a love. It'll make you feel better."

As usual her sister was right, Marci thought as she nuzzled the kitten's soft fur.

THE COOK-OFF WAS GOING WELL. The sisters' sauce was simmering and most of the hard work was done.

"I guess we can sit down and wait until it's time for the judging," Sissy commented, pulling up a couple of metal folding chairs. "Harv, come join us."

Harvey had just meandered in with a hamburger in one hand and a cold beer in the other. "Okay," he said. He ladled a generous portion of sauce onto his burger. "This is great. I think we have a winner."

About thirty minutes after he'd finished his meal, everything went south. For Harvey *and* their chance to win. It was a plummet from optimism to despair.

"I don't feel too good," he said as he doubled over. "In fact, I feel *really* bad." That comment was made prior to a dash for the exit.

Sissy and Marci glanced at each other and then at the exit.

"You'd better go check on him," Marci said. "What, uh…"

"I don't know." Sissy marched over to the stove and sniffed the sauce.

She was about to taste it when Marci intervened. "I don't think you should do that." She told Sissy about her last encounter with Idabelle, and didn't leave out her strange transaction with the woman in the sunglasses.

Sissy immediately caught the connection. "I'll bet she did something when I left to move the kittens."

"I wouldn't be surprised." Marci looked down the aisle at Idabelle's booth, where she was entertaining a cameraman.

"Crap! That means we have to start over, doesn't it?"

"I'm going to throw this out, just to be safe," Marci

said, trying to decide how to dispose of a full Dutch oven of barbecue sauce.

"I agree. If you'll get going on a new batch, I'll check on Harvey. He looked downright green."

THE DAY THAT HAD begun as a disaster ended on a high note. The judges oohed and aahed over their new sauce, which had benefited from a few hastily assembled ingredients and plenty of invention. The beer they'd added at the last minute might have had something to do with it, too. Idabelle made herself scarce during the judging, and the TV cameramen were enchanted by Sissy. Marci could almost smell the leather seats of her new car. Too bad her heart was MIA.

"Are you Marci Hamilton?"

That voice had an edge Marci had always associated with East Coast blue bloods. Not that she'd ever really known one. The woman standing there looked as if she belonged to the voice; she was tiny, brunette, beautiful and wearing enough expensive jewelry to fill a Tiffany's vault.

"Yes, I am." She wanted to add "so what" but managed to refrain. Her good manners seemed to pop up at the most inopportune times.

"You're dating my husband." It was a statement, not a question.

"I don't date married men," Marci said and the temperature in the tent cooled considerably.

"I beg to differ." The woman waved a hand in the air, almost blinding Marci with the glint of the biggest diamond she'd ever seen. "You spent the night with my husband at the Palacio."

Could Johnny be married? Naw. "So you're the

infamous ex-wife I've heard about." *That* should stop her unwanted guest.

Oops. Red face, bulgy eyes—the woman was about to have apoplexy.

Marci was thinking about calling 911 when her un-invited visitor gathered her composure.

"That's a mere technicality. We're going to recon-cile." She dismissed her ex-wife status like it was some kind of pesky servant.

Marci continued to organize the utensils. She would not let the bitch under her skin. Ignore. Ignore. Ignore.

"I suppose sleeping with the boss is an age-old remedy for incompetence."

Try as she might, she couldn't ignore that. Marci gave her a frosty glare. "What are you talking about?"

The woman's throaty laugh sent chills up Marci's spine. "I mean how clichéd is that, having sex with J. W. Watson to win some silly contest."

That was when all the inconsistencies clicked, all the puzzle pieces fell into place, and Marci's world came crashing down. She took one look at the diamonds and couture clothing and knew this woman was telling the truth. Johnny Walker was J. W. Watson. He was the rich and famous J. W. Watson!

When in doubt, and your heart was breaking, it was time to call in the big guns. "Sissy, Sissy!" Marci screamed.

"What, what?" Sissy roared to the rescue.

"She, she, she—" Marci pointed at the ex-Mrs. Watson who was looking more and more unsure. And who could blame her? Sissy, no doubt, seemed entirely capable of mayhem.

"You've been warned. He's merely trifling with you," Marina declared before she scurried away.

"What was that all about?" Sissy asked.

"He's…he's—" Hysteria was no longer nipping at her heels; it had turned into a full-blown monster.

"He betrayed me," Marci sobbed.

"Who betrayed you?"

"Johnny," Marci managed between sobs.

"Oh," Sissy murmured, leading Marci toward a chair. "Just stay there. I'll be right back and you can tell me all about it."

She quickly found Harvey, who was looking considerably better. "I'm taking Marci back to the motel. Call me when they make the announcement about the winners."

"What's wrong?" he asked, perplexed.

"I don't know. Come to the suite as soon as you can. I suspect this is something awful."

"Will do."

The silence on the drive to the motel was broken only by an occasional hiccup.

"What happened?" Sissy asked once they were inside the room.

Marci flopped on the bed and flung an arm over her eyes. "Johnny isn't Johnny and he isn't a poor cowboy."

Sissy sat down next to her. "So… who is he?"

"He's J. W. Watson," Marci sniffled.

"Who?"

"J. W. Watson, remember? The singer? The guy sponsoring this whole thing?" Marci was working her way toward being livid. "I'm gonna *kill* him." She was betrayed, devastated and working on furious. Oh, yeah, Johnny Walker Watson had better watch out.

"Are you kidding me?" Sissy was incredulous. And

why not? By any standard it was an incredible situation. "Tell me you're kidding. That woman told you? Who was she, anyway? And do you actually believe her?"

"His ex-wife, Marina. And, yes, I believe her. Think about it. He has those rich friends. Vince fawned all over him. He didn't have a job and he had that weird habit of wearing sunglasses all the time. You can bet your bottom dollar I believe her. You should've seen her diamonds!"

Marci suddenly jerked up off the bed. "I think she's the woman I saw talking to Idabelle, too! She paid her to sabotage our sauce and keep us from winning. What a bitch!" she exclaimed as she fell back on the bed. "Since Idabelle was probably going to tube us anyway, she got a bonus. Damn!"

"Oh, boy," Sissy moaned. "Oh, boy. This is terrible. Wait a minute! Vince said he had an *ex*-wife. Damn! I should have Googled him, but didn't. So what's Marina doing here?"

"She said they were about to reconcile. I'll reconcile him!" Marci's mad was about to overtake her despair. When she caught up with the guy, she was going to tear him limb from limb. "Do you have any wine?"

"Refrigerator." Sissy waved in the direction of the armoire.

Marci almost ripped the handle off the tiny fridge as she retrieved the bottle and popped the cork. Somewhere it was five o'clock, and who cared, anyway.

"Do you believe that?"

"I don't know," Marci snapped. "I fell in love and he was playing a twisted game. The rich singer was diddling the hick-town kindergarten teacher. Isn't that pitiful?" Then Marci had a terrible thought. "Tell me he wasn't doing this to use for the lyrics in a song."

Sissy threw her hands in the air.

Chapter Twenty-Seven

It was time for some big decisions. Shortly after Marci's meltdown, Harvey had called with some wonderful news. They had won the contest! By gosh, they were the big winners. And even more interesting, Idabelle Cornell's shenanigans had resulted in her being permanently banned from any and all J. W. Watson events—no money, no fame. It was bad karma at its best.

At any rate, Marci was faced with a huge conundrum. Should she stay or should she go home? If she stayed and he showed up for the award ceremony, she might be tempted to murder him. But if she went home, she'd miss the opportunity to pummel Mr. J. W. Watson, a.k.a. Johnny Walker.

Maybe, just maybe, he had an excuse for this fiasco. *That* was probably wishful thinking. If he'd ever, even once, mentioned the *L* word, she'd be tempted to talk to him. But he'd been remarkably silent on the subject of love and commitment. Marci had originally thought that was because he'd had such a bad experience with marriage. Now she wasn't quite so sure.

For her it had to be the whole enchilada—heart and soul, now and forever. Even if he had a good excuse,

Marci was afraid she'd never trust him again. So she was going home. First things first; they had to do an interview with the Nashville Network folks.

Time to doll up, put on a big smile and act excited. If she pulled that off she should get an Oscar nomination.

"ARE YOU POSITIVE you want to do this?" Sissy asked again. "I can take care of it, really."

"No, I'm not about to dump it on you. That wouldn't be fair. Harvey hates the camera."

"That he does." Sissy smiled.

"So let's do the interview." Marci told Sissy she planned to go home before the awards ceremony and her sister had agreed with her decision.

Marci felt very blessed to have such a great sister.

SHE *SHOULD* CONSIDER a career in acting. To the casual observer Marci looked as happy as a clam. Broken hearts obviously didn't show on the outside.

They did a joint interview with Vince, and Sissy flirted with the singer until Marci was afraid Harvey would have a stroke.

Finally, the media ordeal was over. Marci's cheeks ached from smiling and her head was pounding.

"I'm going to the ladies' room. I'll be back in a minute." Actually it was an outhouse.

After she'd finished, she made a detour by one of the vendor tents for a Coke. An icy Coke, full of caffeine and sugar, and a couple of aspirins sounded like heaven.

Marci found an empty picnic table under the shade of an oak. As helpful as Sissy and Harvey had been, she needed to be alone for a few minutes. She had just closed her eyes and was rolling the cold can across her forehead when she felt someone sit down next to her. Johnny.

It had to be Johnny, or J.W. or whatever name he was going by today.

Marci opened her eyes, not sure whether she was going to kiss him or scream at him; however, that turned out to be a moot point. Her visitor wasn't Johnny. It was Pancho!

That did it. "Stop. Stalking. Me." What next—a plague of locusts?

"*Señora,* please don't scream." The man held his hands up in the universe signal for surrender. "And *por favor,* don't let that she-devil get to me. She is *mucho loco.*"

Even though the guy scared the heck out of her, Marci was tempted to laugh at his assessment of Brunhilda. Score one for the good girls. "Okay, what do you want? And keep in mind that I have her on speed dial." Marci held up her cell phone. She wasn't sure he knew what speed dial was, but a threat was a threat. And she didn't have many in her arsenal.

"Señora Hamilton, please let me explain."

Marci waggled the phone at him.

"I work for Señor Bill. My name is Sanchez. I am his ranch manager."

Marci was not only flabbergasted, she was flat-out shocked. Bill?

"You're *what?*"

"Señor Bill, he asked me to keep you safe."

It originated as a giggle and quickly grew into a full-blown laugh. "You mean Bill sent you up here to watch over me?" Marci asked when she'd recovered from her bout of lunacy.

"Sí." Her unwanted bodyguard smiled and slumped against the park bench.

"I thought you were stalking me," Marci said. She couldn't imagine why she was confiding in a guy who could have easily stepped out of a grade B western. "Was Bill calling me on my cell phone?"

"Sí. Our, what do you call it, our service is very bad. Sometimes we have connections, sometimes we have static. Señor Bill, he gets the newspaper from your town, and he read that you and your sister were going driving all over Texas. That made him shrimpy. So I say to him, I will make sure nothing happens."

"Shrimpy?" Bill was over six feet tall.

"You know. He's—" David flapped his hands "—he's, uh, he's—"

"Crabby?"

"Ah, that is the word." Her new friend smiled.

"And why did he think we wouldn't be safe?" Marci was baffled by her ex-boyfriend's motivation.

He shrugged. "He say something about your sister, she not quite so…" The thought remained unsaid.

"Holy moly." The whole scenario had come from so far out in left field, Marci was speechless.

Marina, Bill, Pancho/Sanchez, J. W. Watson—what next? Little green men?

"Let's go across the street to the café and have some coffee," Marci suggested. She planned to feed the guy and send him off with a message for his boss. The problem was, she didn't have a clue what she wanted to say to Bill.

Would *go away and leave me alone* work? Men— she'd had it! As far as she was concerned, they could all take a flying leap.

"Ah, that café is next door to the sheriff's office, is it not?" he murmured.

Big oops! No green card, no legal entry. "Maybe we should find another place," she said as they approached the Coffee Cup.

"Oh, yes, please."

They walked several blocks to a small diner where Sanchez chowed down on a double cheeseburger with extra fries.

"I like hamburgers," he announced. "But now, it is business we need to do." He pulled a cell phone from his pocket. "Señor Bill is expecting our call." He punched in some numbers. "We have new satellite phone."

"Are you joking?" Marci was tempted to let out a primal scream. What was with men trying to run her life?

"Here he is. Señor Bill." David handed her the phone.

"What do you want?" Marci had ditched her manners and morphed into being downright shrimpy.

"I love you and I want you to come to the ranch," he said abruptly. "Sanchez will bring you."

"Oh, Bill." Marci tried to figure out what to say. How about, *I really like you but get the hell out of my life.* No, that was bit harsh. Ditto for *I've fallen in love with someone else.*

So what was her recourse? How about *It's been nice knowing you, but don't contact me again?*

However, before she could say anything, Bill continued the conversation.

"Please, Marci. I'm crazy about you, and I miss you so much. Come to the ranch."

"I can't live the life of a fugitive." Marci shook her head; a feeling of despair was settling on her shoulders. "That wouldn't be fair to my family and it wouldn't be fair to me. Plus…I've met someone I care a great deal about." No need to tell him she thought that relationship had reached a dead end.

"Is he that Johnny Walker guy Sanchez told me about?"

"Yes." He certainly didn't need to know about the J. W. Watson debacle.

"Are you sure?"

"Yes." It was time for a little white lie. "We're planning to get married. Next week, in fact."

"You deserve better than living with some cowboy in a double wide."

And that comment came from an indicted murderer? Marci prayed that God wouldn't strike her dead for her next lie. "He's going to live with me in Port Serenity."

There was a long silence before Bill spoke again. "If you're really happy and you're positive he's the one, I'll reluctantly say I'm pleased. You're very special to me. Always remember that, Marci."

"I will, truly I will."

"What do you mean Marci's gone home?" Johnny was trying to keep from yelling.

When he'd left town, he'd been operating in a state of panic. But he *had* left a note, and he *had* tried to call, several times, in fact.

He'd been about to send Brian to Marfa when he was waylaid by a distressing message from his attorney, Jason Scuggs, concerning Marina. Jason had seen an advance reading copy of her book and it contained some false references to Randy. Did Johnny want to sue to stop production?

Damned right he did!

The minute he got that part of his life straightened out, he'd headed back to Marfa, only to find that the love of his life was gone. Gone! And he didn't have a clue why she'd disappeared—other than that he suspected she'd somehow discovered his identity.

He finally found Sissy and Harvey at the café having breakfast. Unfortunately, Sissy appeared to be his only source of information and she looked like she'd enjoy taking a twelve-gauge shotgun to him.

"What do you *mean* she's gone?" he repeated vehemently.

She gave him a malevolent glare. "I mean she went home so she wouldn't have to deal with a scum-sucking pig like you, that's what I mean."

He was definitely at the top of the sisters' hit list. What could he do about it? Well, before he could fix the problem, he had to figure out exactly what had happened.

"Sissy, please. Tell me what's going on," he pleaded. If it took eating humble pie, he had his fork ready.

"Please," he said again, seeing that she was on the verge of softening. Either that or she was devising a new and insidious kind of torture.

"You heard me, Mr. Watson. My sister doesn't want anything to do with you."

"I left a note on your car. Didn't she get it?" Johnny then explained about Randy's accident and his mad rush out of town.

Sissy and Harvey exchanged glances, but Harvey was the first to speak. "There wasn't any note."

"Of course there was. I stuffed it under your windshield wiper. And then I left a couple of messages on her voicemail."

"The phone messages I can explain. The ditz erased everything without listening to them. What a blonde! But the note—"

Harvey interrupted Sissy. "It was windy that day. I'll bet it's out in the desert."

Damn! "You're probably right. So, does she really not want to see me again, or is she just mad?" Johnny wisely skipped over the issue of his true identity. He figured that was a fight for another day.

Harvey quickly deep sixed that hope. "My sister-in-law met your ex-wife. And believe me, Miss Marci wasn't impressed."

Call him flummoxed. "My ex-wife? She met Marina?" Johnny repeated. He sounded like the village idiot, but did he care? "What nonsense is Marina spouting now?"

"I think the gist of the conversation was that you two were reconciling, and she also dropped the bomb about your identity. I suspect her goal was to break you guys up," Sissy informed him. "And she did a darned fine job of it."

Johnny had to agree.

"I also suspect she was behind Marci's latest phone calls and Idabelle's attempt to sabotage our sauce," Harvey said.

It was time to call Jason again. Johnny had been reluctant to play hardball with Marina because she was Randy's mother. Even during the height of the book fiasco, he hadn't sent his attorney after her on a personal level.

But now she'd gone too far. He had to permanently banish her from his life.

"I'll have my attorney take care of Marina. I'm going to talk to Marci myself and I'll need your assistance."

"Why should we help you? At best you were duplicitous, and at worst you were toying with my sister's affections." Sissy had segued from a glare to a sneer.

Maybe that was an improvement, maybe not.

"I love her and I plan to ask her to marry me," he declared.

"Oh, my," Sissy muttered. "That does make a difference." She nodded. " It makes a *huge* difference."

"What do you think, Harv?" Johnny asked.

"I think that if we get involved and you mess with Marci's feelings, your life won't be worth spit."

"That's for sure," Sissy piped up. "I can personally guarantee it."

"I love her. I promise I won't hurt her."

"You already have."

"I know, and that was one of the stupidest things I've ever done. At the time I thought I was handling it right. I realize now I shouldn't have lied about who I am—or anything else."

Harvey turned to Sissy, who shrugged. "Well, Johnny, my boy. Looks like we need to come up with a battle plan and it better be a good one 'cause she's a tough cookie."

Truer words were never spoken.

Chapter Twenty-Eight

Marci had been back in Port Serenity a week, and she was crankier than a woman with a hot flash. Lolly, Christian and the kids—minus the twins—had been doing the tiptoe-on-eggshells routine. It was stupid to feel the way she did, especially since they were trying to be kind, but she couldn't help herself. All those "poor Mee Maw" looks made her want to throw up. Not even her sunshine-yellow VW convertible could lift her spirits.

The only bright spot was Sissy had told her all about Randy's accident and Johnny's attempt to contact her. That miscommunication was partially her fault. But, and it was a *big* but, he hadn't even made an attempt to contact her since she returned to Port Serenity. If all else failed, he could have used Western Union, or a sky-writer or a carrier pigeon. But did he do anything?

Nope! Not. One. Single. Thing.

And to make matters worse, ever since Sissy and Harvey got back from Marfa they'd been acting like newlyweds. It seemed that Sissy was using Vince's crush on her to get Harvey to make a commitment, and when he did, she told the country star to take a hike. If that didn't beat all!

So now they were all kissy-face, snookums, huggy-wuggy. It was enough to make you sick. Why didn't they just get married? Oh right, they did. On the way home they'd made a detour through one of the Las Vegas wedding chapels. Darn it! They hadn't even asked her to be their matron of honor. Marci would've gone to Vegas, honestly she would.

Only Sissy could have managed to sneak Mama Cat and her two remaining babies into the Bellagio. The other kittens had been adopted in West Texas. When she put her mind to it, Sissy could be very persuasive. And speaking of the kittens, Shirley and her brother Cecil ran through the living room chasing a ball of twine. Darn, they were cute.

MARCI DIDN'T KNOW IT, but several days after she got home, Johnny contacted Lolly, resulting in a conference call that had also included Christian, Sissy, Harvey, C.J. and Olivia. With Sissy's assurance that he was thoroughly repentant, the gang formulated The Plan. If it bombed, half the people in Port Serenity would incur Marci's wrath.

"Will this really work?" It was the fourth time Johnny had asked Brian the same question and his patient business manager looked like he was about to suggest a long walk off a short pier.

"I can't guarantee she'll take you back even if you're able to pull off this stunt. What I can guarantee is that this will be a memorable marriage proposal."

"I guess that's all I can ask." Johnny leaned back in his desk chair and reached for his glass of Scotch. "Are you absolutely positive everything's ready?"

"Aaaggh!"

"I get it. Everything will be fine." During the past week he'd talked to Lolly at least a dozen times.

Putting together this type of project was a logistical nightmare. Thank goodness he had Brian, aka Mr. Marvel, on his side.

"Do you think she'll say yes?"

Brian gave a disgusted grunt, and Randy broke into gales of laughter.

"Okay, I get it. I'm obsessing and I need to stop."

"Yeah!" they agreed in unison.

THE WEEK TURNED into the weekend, and Marci didn't feel a darned bit better. But she could put on a good face with the best of them. "What else do you need me to do?" she asked as she bounced Dana on her lap. The other twin was asleep in her swing.

"I've got everything under control. Entertaining the girls is a big help," Lolly said as she pulled a huge casserole of baked beans out of the oven.

Christian and Bren were outside cooking burgers on the grill. Sunday lunch had always been a special family time, but there was something out of the ordinary going on. Marci just couldn't put her finger on what it was.

"Why do you have so much food?" she asked. Lolly had fixed enough to feed the entire town.

"Didn't I tell you? Aunt Sissy and Uncle Harvey are coming over. I also invited C.J., Olivia and a couple of people you haven't seen in a while. I thought we'd celebrate Sissy and Harvey's wedding."

"Speaking of Sissy, I haven't seen her lately."

"Really? I talked to her last night and she said she'd be here today. She's busy being a newlywed."

"I guess you're right." Marci jumped when she heard a big bang.

"What's all that noise outside?"

Lolly responded by turning up the radio.

"I'm going to take a look." Marci started to get up but Lolly stopped her.

"It's probably Bren and his friends. They're playing football on the front lawn."

"I thought Bren was helping Christian cook."

"He is."

"That doesn't make any sense."

Their conversation was abbreviated when Sissy and Harvey strolled in the kitchen. Harvey kissed Marci's cheek, while Sissy went over and fiddled with the radio. What were they doing? The salsa music was already so loud Marci could barely hear herself think.

"How's my favorite sister-in-law?" Harv shouted.

"Fine, Harv." Marci returned the shout and grinned at her new brother-in-law. "How's married life?"

"Great," he replied. "Let me show you something." He pulled Sissy over and proudly displayed her hand, which was sporting a huge rock. "We bought cheap rings in Vegas. So I went into Houston and got my sweetie a genuine diamond."

"Wow!" Marci squealed so loudly the twins woke up and joined in the festivities. The radio was blasting, the babies were howling and the adults were in celebration mode. It was complete bedlam.

Marci could feel her blue funk lift and she was still grinning when C.J. and Olivia arrived.

"Whoa, party time," C.J. said as he gave both Marci and Sissy a kiss.

"Lolly, why is the music so—" Lolly's frown stopped Olivia's question in midsentence.

"Why *is* the music so loud?" Marci asked.

"Because there are some songs I want to hear," Lolly answered and turned it up another notch.

That was downright rude. What had happened to her daughter's manners?

"I need to go outside and check on something," Lolly said.

Before anyone could reply she was out the back door.

"I'll go help her," C.J. proclaimed.

Help her with what?

"So, what do you think about the stock market?" Harvey asked, not actually addressing his question to anyone.

Something was definitely up, and everyone was in on it.

"Mee Maw, you wanna come up to my room and see my new cell phone?"

Even Amanda was a conspirator.

When Christian and Bren hurried in wearing matching grins, the hair prickled on the back of Marci's neck. She studied the faces of the people she loved. Amanda was about to burst and the rest of them had guilty faces.

Although Christian snapped off the radio, the music continued. Not only did it continue, it was loud and it came from outside.

"What *is* going on?"

"Let's go out on the front porch," Christian suggested.

"Yeah, Mee Maw, let's go out on the porch." Amanda was dancing in place as she grabbed Marci's hand and urged her toward the door. How could Marci resist that?

As she got closer to the front of the house, Marci heard something she hadn't noticed in the kitchen—general crowd noise. What in the name of heaven was happening?

"Look. Look at that!" Amanda exclaimed, throwing open the door.

Good Lord, there were people everywhere. People in the street. People in Lolly's yard. People sitting on cars. It looked like most of the folks in Port Serenity had taken a leisurely Sunday drive to Lolly's neighborhood.

Astonishing as that was, it wasn't nearly as amazing as the band on the improvised stage of a flatbed eighteen wheeler.

"That's Johnny," she muttered. "Johnny's out there." Marci whirled around to stare at her family, who had expanded their circle to include Brian and Randy.

Sure enough, they were all wearing the same goofy grins.

"Mama, look." Lolly pointed at the stage.

Johnny stepped up to the microphone and started to sing.

Marci had desperately missed her sexy, funny, lovable cowboy with the velvet baritone. His voice alone could make her melt. Add his smile and she was a goner. Just ask anyone in the audience; they were all mesmerized as he sang song after song.

Mrs. Pomerantz and her buddy Gladys were up front grooving to the music.

"How did you pull this off?"

Lolly waved at the crowd. "Mrs. Pomerantz put it on the grapevine, and voilà, there you have it."

Marci was astonished. How had she missed the gossip?

"Think about it, Mama. You've been pretty much out of the loop lately."

When Johnny finished the last tune, he strolled to the front of the improvised stage.

"Marci Hamilton," he boomed. His microphone-enhanced voice could've been heard in Corpus. "I love you. *I love you."* Following that proclamation, he got down on one knee.

Marci vacillated between a grin and a wince. When you got to a certain age you didn't plop down on a knee without a lot of forethought.

"I'm really sorry I didn't tell you the truth."

The crowd had grown silent.

"Please," he went on, "put me out of my misery and marry me."

Her friends and neighbors cheered and turned en masse to stare at Marci.

Merciful heavens! How could she *not* love him? No matter what kind of misunderstandings they'd had in the past, they could work out their problems. If you cared enough, that was what you did. Marci took a tentative step toward the stage and before she knew it the crowd had parted and she was running toward the man she loved.

How could any girl, from sixteen to sixty, resist that kind of proposal?

With the help of her friends, Marci Hamilton climbed aboard the improvised stage.

"Oh, Johnny. Yes! Yes, I'll marry you," she said as she got down on her knees, too.

"Thank goodness," he muttered before he thrust his fingers through her hair and engaged her in a long, long kiss.

Of course the crowd stomped, and yelled, and exhibited a Texas-size appreciation for love.

"Are you thinking what I'm thinking?" Marci asked when she'd managed to stop grinning.

"You bet. So what do we do?"

"Give me the microphone," she said and then made an announcement.

"Someone needs to winch us up!"

Epilogue

"I'm so nervous I'm about to die," Marci said, half-heartedly resisting the urge to check the mirror *again*. It wasn't every day a girl got married. And it certainly wasn't normal for half the folks in the Country Music Hall of Fame to be sitting in Lolly's front yard.

"You're absolutely gorgeous. So stop fiddling around. Johnny's waiting for you."

Sissy was the ultimate in bossy, but this time she was right. Never in her wildest dreams had Marci imagined she'd find the second love of her life—especially not when the discovery resulted from one of Sissy's hare-brained schemes.

"Come on, Mee Maw, let's go."

Amanda looked angelic in her pink sundress. When Marci had asked her favorite females—Lolly, Olivia, Sissy and Amanda—to be her attendants, she'd told them they could wear anything they wanted. Her only criterion had been that they dress appropriately for a garden wedding. And here they were, resembling a bouquet of summer flowers—even Sissy.

It all felt like a dream. Lolly and Sissy had accompanied her to Houston on her now-infamous dress-buying trip. They meant well, but they drove her crazy.

Too tight. Too loose. Too much cleavage. Not enough cleavage. Too white. Too yellow. Yikes!

Marci had finally had it with their bickering and sent them off to have a margarita. When she could look around without the helpful duo, she found the perfect outfit—an off-the-shoulder cream silk sheath. It was elegant, understated and gorgeous.

In the background she could hear Vince McDowell singing. That was her cue.

"Let's do it," she said.

Marci stopped briefly on the front porch to survey the miraculous transformation of Lolly's front lawn to her wedding chapel. Then she scanned the sea of guests and locked eyes with Johnny, her Johnny. He smiled, and all her nervousness melted away. She returned his smile and walked down the steps into her new life.

"HOW LONG DO WE HAVE to stay to be polite?" Johnny kissed the side of her neck. "We have a honeymoon to get started," he said, oblivious to the fact that Randy had joined them.

"Marcela, you've outdone yourself with this reception." The voice could belong to none other than Mrs. Pomerantz. Her ever-present buddy, Gladys Schmidt, was right behind her. The two ladies barreled up carrying plates of barbecue.

Yes, Texas barbecue. And you could blame Brian for that one. He wanted to test all the new sauces the company had produced as a result of the cook-off.

"I'm glad you're enjoying yourself. Have you met Johnny and his son, Randy?"

"You are such a handsome young man." Mrs. Pomerantz emphasized her point by pinching Randy's cheek. "And I am such a J. W. Watson fan," she gushed. "Would you sign this?" She pushed a napkin at Johnny.

"I'd be pleased to," he replied, and as he gave her back the piece of paper, he kissed her hand.

Swear to goodness, Marci expected the woman to expire on the spot.

"Ladies, if you'll excuse us, I see someone Johnny and I need to speak to." She pulled her new husband through the crowd toward the backyard.

"Where are we heading?"

"We're going to find someplace private because I need a kiss."

"Glad to oblige, ma'am," he said flashing her one of those grins that promised more interesting events than a mere kiss.

He looped an arm over her shoulder as he drew her toward a bower of bougainvillea. "I have to warn you. Ardent fans are part of my job," he said. "In small groups they're great. It's when you're faced with a crowd that it gets a bit old."

Marci grinned, and Johnny knew exactly what she was thinking.

"Just like barbecue," they said in unison, and broke into gales of laughter.

* * * * *

Turn the page for a sneak preview of
IF I'D NEVER KNOWN YOUR LOVE
by
Georgia Bockoven

From the brand-new series
Harlequin Everlasting Love
Every great love has a story to tell. ™

One year, five months and four days missing

There's no way for you to know this, Evan, but I haven't written to you for a few months. Actually, it's been almost a year. I had a hard time picking up a pen once more after we paid the second ransom and then received a letter saying it wasn't enough. I was so sure you were coming home that I took the kids along to Bogotá so they could fly home with you and me, something I swore I'd never do. I've fallen in love with Colombia and the people who've opened their hearts to me. But fear is a constant companion when I'm there. I won't ever expose our children to that kind of danger again.

I'm at a loss over what to do anymore, Evan. I've begged and pleaded and thrown temper tantrums with every official I can corner both here and at home. They've been incredibly tolerant and understanding, but in the end as ineffectual as the rest of us.

I try to imagine what your life is like now, what you do every day, what you're wearing, what you eat. I want to believe that the people who have you are misguided yet kind, that they treat you well. It's how I survive day to day. To think of you being mistreated hurts too much. If I picture you locked away somewhere and suffering, a weight descends on me that makes it almost impossible to get out of bed in the morning.

Your captors surely know you by now. They have to recognize what a good man you are. I imagine you working with their children, telling them that you have children, too, showing them the pictures you carry in your wallet. Can't the men who have you understand how much your children miss you? How can it not matter to them?

How can they keep you away from us all this time? Over and over, we've done what they asked. Are they oblivious to the depth of their cruelty? What kind of people are they that they don't care?

I used to keep a calendar beside our bed next to the peach rose you picked for me before you left. Every night I marked another day, counting how many you'd been gone. I don't do that any longer. I don't want to be reminded of all the days we'll never get back.

When I can't sleep at night, I tell you about my day. I imagine you hearing me and smiling over the details that make up my life now. I never tell you how defeated I feel at moments or how hard I work to hide it from everyone for fear they will see it as a reason to stop believing you are coming home to us.

And I couldn't tell you about the lump I found in my breast and how difficult it was going through all the tests without you here to lean on. The lump was benign—the process reaching that diagnosis utterly terrifying. I couldn't stop thinking about what would happen to Shelly and Jason if something happened to me.

We need you to come home.

I'm worn down with missing you.

I'm going to read this tomorrow and will probably tear it up or burn it in the fireplace. I don't want you to get the idea I ever doubted what I was doing to free you or thought the work a burden. I would gladly spend the rest of my life at it, even if, in the end, we only had one day together.

You are my life, Evan.

I will love you forever.

* * * * *

Don't miss this deeply moving
Harlequin Everlasting Love story
about a woman's struggle to bring back
her kidnapped husband from Colombia
and her turmoil over whether to let go,
finally, and welcome another man into her life.
IF I'D NEVER KNOWN YOUR LOVE
by Georgia Bockoven
is available March 27, 2007.

And also look for
THE NIGHT WE MET
by Tara Taylor Quinn,
a story about finding love
when you least expect it.

nocturne™

IT'S TIME TO DISCOVER
THE RAINTREE TRILOGY...

There have always been those among us
who are more than human...

Don't miss the dramatic first book by

New York Times bestselling author

LINDA
HOWARD

RAINTREE:
Inferno

On sale May.

Raintree: Haunted by **Linda Winstead Jones**
Available June.

Raintree: Sanctuary by **Beverly Barton**
Available July.

HARLEQUIN Romance®

presents a brand-new trilogy by

PATRICIA THAYER

Rocky Mountain
BRIDES

Three sisters come home to wed.

In April don't miss

Raising the Rancher's Family,

followed by

The Sheriff's Pregnant Wife,

on sale May 2007,

and

A Mother for the Tycoon's Child,

on sale June 2007.

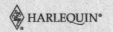

REQUEST YOUR FREE BOOKS!
2 FREE NOVELS PLUS 2
FREE GIFTS!

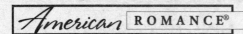

Heart, Home & Happiness!

YES! Please send me 2 FREE Harlequin American Romance® novels and my 2 FREE gifts. After receiving them, if I don't wish to receive any more books, I can return the shipping statement marked "cancel." If I don't cancel, I will receive 4 brand-new novels every month and be billed just $4.24 per book in the U.S., or $4.99 per book in Canada, plus 25¢ shipping and handling per book and applicable taxes, if any*. That's a savings of close to 15% off the cover price! I understand that accepting the 2 free books and gifts places me under no obligation to buy anything. I can always return a shipment and cancel at any time. Even if I never buy another book from Harlequin, the two free books and gifts are mine to keep forever.

154 HDN EEZK 354 HDN EEZV

Name	(PLEASE PRINT)	
Address		Apt. #
City	State/Prov.	Zip/Postal Code

Signature (if under 18, a parent or guardian must sign)

Mail to the **Harlequin Reader Service®**:
IN U.S.A.: P.O. Box 1867, Buffalo, NY 14240-1867
IN CANADA: P.O. Box 609, Fort Erie, Ontario L2A 5X3

Not valid to current Harlequin American Romance subscribers.

Want to try two free books from another line?
Call 1-800-873-8635 or visit www.morefreebooks.com.

* Terms and prices subject to change without notice. NY residents add applicable sales tax. Canadian residents will be charged applicable provincial taxes and GST. This offer is limited to one order per household. All orders subject to approval. Credit or debit balances in a customer's account(s) may be offset by any other outstanding balance owed by or to the customer. Please allow 4 to 6 weeks for delivery.

Your Privacy: Harlequin is committed to protecting your privacy. Our Privacy Policy is available online at www.eHarlequin.com or upon request from the Reader Service. From time to time we make our lists of customers available to reputable firms who may have a product or service of interest to you. If you would prefer we not share your name and address, please check here. ☐

HAR07

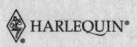

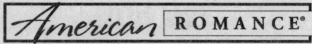

COMING NEXT MONTH

#1157 FROM TEXAS, WITH LOVE by Cathy Gillen Thacker
The McCabes: Next Generation
Will McCabe arrives in New York City with specific instructions—bring
Samantha Holmes back to Laramie, Texas, for her estranged brother's wedding.
Convincing the fiery brunette to come back with him is one thing.... But Will
realizes he wants her to stay in Laramie for good—and convincing her to do
that is another thing altogether.

#1158 NINE MONTHS' NOTICE by Michele Dunaway
American Beauties
After waiting two years for her perfect man to commit, Tori Adams has decided it's
time to move on. She wants it all—marriage, family, career—and if Jeff Wright
isn't interested, then neither is she! But when Tori discovers she's pregnant, will
nine months' notice change his mind?

#1159 IT HAPPENED ONE WEDDING by Ann Roth
To Wed, or Not To Wed
After the cancellation of her own nuptials a year ago, events planner
Cammie Yarnell avoids planning weddings at the Oceanside B & B. But now a
dear friend wants to get married there and Cammie can't refuse to help, even
though it means working with Curt Blanco—her ex-fiancé's best friend, and the
man who helped ruin her wedding plans!

#1160 THE RIGHT TWIN by Laura Marie Altom
Times Two
Impersonating her twin sister for a weekend should be a piece of cake for
Sarah Connelly. What could go wrong? Running a successful inn isn't as easy
as she thought it would be, though, especially when she falls for a sexy guest!
Heath Brown is perfect for her, but what Sarah doesn't realize is that Heath has
a few secrets of his own....

www.eHarlequin.com

HARCNM0307